PUPS, PUMPKINS, AND MURDER

a Samantha Davies mystery

S.A. Kazlo

For the three rays of sunshine in my life—Max, Cody and Sarah—I love you all to the moon and back.

WINGS FALLS

A. SWEETIE PIE'S CAFÉ
B. THE CLOTHES HORSE
C. THE SMILING PIG
D. THE SOUND MACHINE
E. THE TOY BOX
F. SAINT ANTHONY'S CATHOLIC CHURCH
G. CIVIL WAR MONUMENT
H. THE EWE AND ME WOOLERY
I. MOMMA MIA'S
J. THE NUT HOUSE
K. WINGS FALLS LIBRARY
L. WINGS FALLS PARK
M. AL'S FLY SHOP
N. TOP DRAWER CONSIGNMENTS
O. CANDIE PARKER- HOGAN'S HOME
P. WINGS FALLS SENIOR CENTER
Q. WINGS FALLS POLICE STATION
R. WINGS FALL COMMUNITY COLLEGE
S. SHOP AND SAVE
T. SAMANTHA DAVIES' HOME
U. WINGS FALLS ANIMAL HOSPITAL

Acknowledgements

I owe a great deal of gratitude to June Kosier, Margie Ortega and my Thursday night critique group for helping bring this book to life—Zachary Richards, Robin Inwald, Sandy Buxton, Montana Tracey, Kay Hafner, and Billy Neary. Thank you all so very much.

I'm forever grateful to my publisher, Gemma Halliday, for believing in me, Sam, Candie, and Porkchop. Thank you.

Thank you to Jennifer Rarden for whipping this book into shape. And for my biggest cheerleader and believing in me, my husband, Michael. I love you.

My readers, thank you from the bottom of my heart for taking the time to enter my little world of Wings Fall and its characters.

CHAPTER ONE

———

Who knew a pumpkin could kill a person? I was sure Scooter Dickenson never thought his prize-winning 2,000-pound gourd would be the means of a person's death when his flatbed truck rumbled into the Wings Falls Park yesterday morning. The victim—Edgar Jensen—was the new loan officer at the Wings Falls National Bank. I had never met Edgar before yesterday, when I had the misfortune of making his acquaintance at the annual Taste of Wings Falls Fair. I say misfortune because from what I observed at the fair, he wasn't the nicest person, arguing with a number of fairgoers. But was someone mad enough at Edgar to want him dead? These questions ran through my mind as I sat with my cousin, Candie, in our regular booth in Sweetie Pie's Café after Sunday Mass at Saint Anthony's.

The weekend had started off wonderfully.

*   *   *

It was Friday night, and my boyfriend Hank Johnson, Candie, and her new hubby Mark Hogan, and I were sitting in Adirondack chairs around the metal fire pit in my backyard enjoying s'mores and mugs of hot chocolate. I was mesmerized by the flames licking the oak logs in the circle of fire as they reached for the sky. The sparks reminded me of the lightning bugs flitting around that I would try to capture on a summer night when I was a child.

Earlier in the afternoon, I had walked my reddish-brown dachshund, Porkchop, through the maze of tents set up for the Wings Falls annual fall event—A Taste of Wings Falls. Vendors were busy preparing to sell everything from wool scarves to maple syrup. The rug hooking group I belong to, the Loopy Ladies, was going to sell hand-hooked items.

A big draw every year for the Taste was Scooter Dickenson's award-winning pumpkin. As I'd walked close to the flatbed holding this year's beauty, a growl rumbled from deep within Porkchop. I'd looked down, and the short hairs on his back had been standing on end. He'd started to bark and pull on his leash. His behavior had surprised me. If a squirrel had run across our path, I could have understood his agitation, but a pumpkin? Go figure.

"Your marshmallow is going to burn to a crisp if you don't pay attention."

I laughed and pulled the stick holding my charcoal-black marshmallow out of the flames. My Southern Belle cousin, Candie, was right. It was a bit crispy, but then again, that's how I liked my s'mores—a crispy blackened marshmallow sandwiched between a chocolate bar and two graham crackers. I assembled my gooey treat then bit into it. With my eyes closed, a smile of appreciation for the sweet goodness resting on my tongue spread across my face.

"That good, huh?"

My eyes snapped open at my boyfriend's comment. Hank and I had been a couple for a little over a year now, but it wasn't until Candie married Mark, our town's mayor, this past July that he said the "L" word to me at their wedding. When Hank and I met, he was newly transferred to Wings Falls from Albany PD. How we met wasn't the best of circumstances. Porkchop, my main man at the time, and I had stumbled on a dead body. Hank was an investigating officer in the murder of the pet shelter's owner where I was trying to donate a bag of dog food Porkchop had turned his nose up at. A good deed that turned disastrous for me since I became the main suspect in the crime.

I fingered the gold heart-shaped locket hanging around my neck Hank gave me at my cousin's wedding when he proclaimed his love for me. I wore it every day. Warmth spread through me whenever I thought of that special moment.

Porkchop lay at my feet chewing on his favorite treat—a rawhide bone. Nina, Hank's sweet bulldog, curled next to him doing the same. I snuggled into my down vest. The evening's temperatures had dropped since this morning, when the weather was unusually warm for late October.

"How did setting up the Loopy Ladies' booth at the Taste go today?" Hank asked, sipping his hot chocolate from a Harry Potter mug.

Mark and Candie had brought a thermos of hot chocolate, while I supplied the makings for s'mores.

I licked a glob of sticky marshmallow off my fingers. "I think it's as done as it's going to be. Especially with Gladys and Helen overseeing which rug should go where."

Hank laughed. "I can see my aunt now. She'd puff up if Helen Garber didn't agree with her about how your booth should look."

Gladys O'Malley was Hank's octogenarian aunt, my next-door neighbor, and a fellow rug hooker of mine and Candie's. Helen was also a member of the Loopy Ladies. The two strong-minded ladies often butted heads. Neither wanted to give an inch when they spoke their minds. And now that the Loopy Ladies had reserved a booth at the Taste of Wings Falls, held in the town park of my hometown, they each had their own opinion as to how the rugs the members of our group had created should be displayed.

Candie's auburn curls bounced about her shoulders as she shook her head. "I've seen polecats act better when attacking a piece of meat than those two ladies."

I poured more hot chocolate from Candie's thermos into my "Hookers Do It Better" mug. The hot liquid helped warm the parts of me not facing the fire. "I agree with you. If it wasn't for the money we'll raise from the mug rugs and hooked rugs we plan to sell for the benefit of Camp Adirondack, I'd have said the heck with the whole thing." Camp Adirondack was a summer camp that hosted inner city kids during the summer.

Mark raised an eyebrow. "What are mug rugs? Rugs shaped like a mug of beer?"

I laughed. "No, coasters, really. A small, hooked mat to place your mug of coffee or whatever your drink of choice is on so you don't mar the top of your table."

"Okay, gotcha. I think you hookers have a language all of your own."

Candie slapped Mark's arm. "Honey, you don't know the half of it. We hookers are very talented people."

Mark squeezed Candie's hand. "I'm learning that, sweetheart."

Hank leaned forward in his wooden Adirondack chair and scratched between Nina's ears. My fingers itched to push back the lock of brown hair that had a mind of its own and constantly fell onto his forehead. "Mark, how's your campaign for reelection coming? I know you're running unopposed right now, but I'm sure there are things you need to do to make sure people vote for you."

Mark handed a perfectly toasted and melty s'more to Candie. "Right now, things are fine, but I still have to let the people of Wings Falls know what actions I plan to continue for the good of our city. I won't take any vote for granted. There could always be a write-in candidate on election day." He rubbed his forehead and said, "Although he isn't actively campaigning, Bret Hargrove is still on the ballot."

I groaned. Just months ago, Bret was also running for mayor, but his vision of expanding Wings Falls didn't meet with the favor of a lot of the town's citizens. Plus, his being arrested for passing bad checks and using stolen credit cards to fund his campaign didn't help his cause. But some people still believed his lies that he was framed and would vote for him.

Candie bit into her s'more then placed the unfinished portion on the arm of her Adirondack chair. She reached over and clasped Mark's hand in hers. "Now, sweetie, don't go worrying yourself into a stew over this. Wings Falls' citizens are way too smart to fall for that scoundrel's fibs." She raised his hand to her lips and kissed it tenderly. Mark's cheeks reddened, and not from the heat of the roaring fire we sat around or the chill wind that stirred the flames. Mark had pursued my cousin for five years until he finally broke down her one-date policy she had set after breaking off her eleventh engagement. Candie was a natural beauty, with her violet eyes, porcelain skin, and auburn curls that fell to her shoulders. Mark was besotted with her from the first day she came to work as his part-time secretary at city hall.

To turn the conversation back to a lighter subject, I asked, "Who do you think will take home the trophy for the best barbeque in the Wings Falls Barbeque Contest?"

Hank spoke up. "It's going to be a difficult one. We now have three great barbeque restaurants in Wings Fall—Sweetie Pie's, The Round Up, and The Smiling Pig."

Mark rubbed his stomach and licked his lips. "I have no idea who I'm going to cast my vote for, but I know I'm going to enjoy trying to find out."

We all laughed at Mark's statement. It certainly was going to be a tight contest. Franny Goodway owned Sweetie Pie's Café. She moved north a little over fifteen years ago from the south about the same time Candie moved to Wings Falls from Hainted Holler, Tennessee after breaking up with fiancé number eleven. Sweetie Pie's was where a person went for delicious home-cooked food with a Southern touch thrown in. The Round Up was a country western–themed restaurant that opened in the 1950s. Along with its great barbeque, in the evening you could dance to country bands. Back in the day, the restaurant saw the likes of Dolly, Willie, Crystal, and many more now famous singers gracing its stage. The newest barbeque kid on the block was The Smiling Pig, owned by Clint Higgins. In fact, one of the members of the Loopy Ladies, Marybeth Higgins, was his sister.

Mark shook his head. The tassel on the knitted hat pulled over his thinning hair waggled back and forth. "Since we frequent all three of those great restaurants, I don't know how I'm going to make up my mind. I'm glad it's a voter's choice done by secret ballot and I don't have to be a judge."

Porkchop stirred at my feet. He had lain there all evening chewing on his rawhide bone while we all enjoyed our s'mores and hot chocolate.

"It is going to be a tough one, that's for sure."

Hank's phone rang. He pulled it from the pocket of the blue fleece pullover that matched the color of his eyes and swiped the screen. "Hi, Jake. What's up? He did what? I'll be right there. Thanks for the call."

CHAPTER TWO

———

Hank gritted his teeth and shoved the phone back into his pocket. "Sorry, Sam, but I'm going to have to call it an early night." He rose from his chair and looked down at me with regret clouding his eyes.

I reached up and grabbed his hand. "What's happened? Did someone get hurt?" I felt the nervous knot in my stomach I got every time a call came in and he had to leave.

Hank shook his head. His wayward curl fell back onto his forehead. "No, but I feel like pounding some sense into Aaron's head. That was Jake Booker, the owner of The Dugout."

"What did Aaron do?" I was afraid of what Hank would say.

"He walked into The Dugout having already had a few drinks too many. Jake refused to serve him, and Aaron got mouthy. I'm grateful Jake thought to call me."

Aaron was Hank's little brother and Hank's clone—the same wavy dark hair, crystal blue eyes, and tall, muscular build. Unlike Hank, though, Aaron was the spoiled baby of the family, the youngest of seven children, Hank was the oldest. With his good looks, Aaron had charmed his way through life so far, but at twenty-one, he still had a lot of growing up to do. As a teenager, he had started to hang out with an unsavory group, and once he'd reached drinking age, he'd closed down more than one bar. Hank's dear mother had had enough of Aaron's shenanigans and two months ago sent him to live with Hank, hoping his older brother would be a good influence and help straighten him out.

Mark put down his mug of hot chocolate and started to rise out of his chair. "Would you like some company?"

"Thanks buddy, but I can handle this. He won't be the first drunk I gave a ride home to. But this one isn't going to get any sympathy from me."

I knew how hard Hank was trying to help his brother become a good person. He'd given Aaron a roof over his head, put food on the table, and even cosigned an auto loan for him. I didn't know if I would have had the patience Hank did with his younger sibling. "I thought he was doing pretty good staying out of trouble since he moved here?"

"He has. He got a job working at Sweetie Pie's in the kitchen. He was even talking about signing up for the culinary school at the local community college for the winter term. He might be an older student, but a lot of people don't start school right out of high school. Aaron even mentioned going out with Franny's niece, Joy."

Joy worked at her aunt's restaurant to help with her college expenses. She had been attending college down South but decided not to return this fall semester.

I turned to my cousin. "Candie, remember the other day when we stopped into Sweetie Pie's for breakfast? Franny mentioned Joy was going to transfer to Wings Falls Community College for the winter term. I wonder if Aaron had anything to do with her decision. She certainly would be a good influence on him."

Candie licked melted chocolate off her slender fingers. "Yes, she did. Maybe there's more to their romance than we suspect. Hank, you should march that brother of yours to the woodshed for a good talking to." Candie's violet eyes sparkled with mischief. "If you know what I mean."

A grin spread across Hank's five o'clock–shadowed face. "Yes, I do, but he's a tad bigger than me now, so I don't think I could get away with that."

I laughed at Hank's statement. Aaron towered over Hank's six feet by a good four inches.

Nina stirred at his feet. She had been curled up next to Porkchop, chewing on her own rawhide bone. "Could Nina spend the night? I don't know what I'll be dealing with once I get to The Dugout, and I don't want to have to worry about her, too."

I bent and scratched Nina between the ears. "No problem. You know Nina and Porkie are BFFs."

Hank kissed me on the cheek. "I'm sorry to break up this evening. I was really enjoying myself."

Candie waved her ringed fingers at Hank. "Oh, give her a proper kiss."

My laughter at my cousin's smart remark was cut short when Hank pulled me out of my chair and gathered me into his arms. He placed a kiss on my lips that melted my bones.

Candie smiled. "Now that's more like it."

"Walk me to my car," Hank whispered into my ear.

I nodded and grabbed his hand. "Be back in a minute," I called over my shoulder to the newlyweds.

When we stood next to Hank's Jeep, he pressed me against the car door and kissed me again. Thank heavens I was leaning against the car, or I would have slid to the ground. "Take that as a raincheck with more to come." His breath came out in ragged breaths as he weaved his fingers through my curly hair.

I ran a finger along his lips. "Oh, I expect to claim it and soon."

"I guess I better get going. Who knows what my brother is up to, but he will definitely know I'm unhappy with him interrupting my night with you." Hank opened the Jeep's door and climbed in.

I waved goodbye to him as he pulled out of my driveway. My heart went out to him and his problems with his brother. This was one time I figured I was lucky to be an only child, no sibling issues to have to deal with.

Leaves crunched under my suede boots as I walked to my backyard. Mark stood and held out a hand to Candie to help her up. She reached out a hand to me. "Sweetie, I think we'll call it a night, too. We have a big day tomorrow with the Taste of Wings Falls and all the activities going on."

"Yes. I have to get Porkchop's costume ready for the Pet Parade. Then there's all the vendors to check out, and Scooter Dickenson has brought in the pumpkin he grew on his farm."

Mark wrapped an arm around Candie's shoulder. "He grew the largest pumpkin in the county this year. It weighs over two thousand pounds."

I laughed. "Remember the pumpkins we used to grow on Memaw Parker's farm?" Like me, Candie was an only child. Our Memaw and Grandpop Parker raised her on their farm in Hainted Holler after her parents were killed in an automobile accident when she was only five years old. I looked forward to my summers. My parents would send me south to keep Candie company. We'd spend the summer days on the farm running through the fields and daydreaming in the hayloft of their barn. At night, Memaw Parker would hand us each a canning jar and we'd try to catch fireflies.

Firelight sparkled off the ring-laden fingers Candie waved at me. My cousin never met a gem or rhinestone she wasn't in love with. "And I thought *those* pumpkins were big. Scooter has them beat by a mile. I saw it as we drove over here. He has it perched on the end of a flatbed in Wings Falls Park."

I bent and stroked Porkchop. "Yes, Porkchop and I saw it, too, when we went for a walk this afternoon."

"Yeah, there's going to be an official weighing of the big boy before the festival ends," Mark said.

Candie tightened her purple wool scarf around her neck to ward off the chill breeze that was picking up. Purple was Candie's color of choice, from her painted purple Victorian home to her violet eyes. "That's right. For a dollar you can take a chance on the pumpkin's exact weight then find it out tomorrow night when all the festivities are over. The winner will get half of the proceeds. The rest will go to Camp Adirondack."

"I hope that, along with the rugs and coasters the Loopy Ladies have hooked, will bring in a lot of money. It would mean more inner-city kids could spend a few weeks enjoying our beautiful mountains."

I crossed my fingers and wished for tomorrow's success. The mountains surrounding the lakes and villages where I lived in Upstate New York were breathtaking and a far cry from the skyscrapers and crowds of the inner city.

I waggled my fingers at Mark and Candie to shoo them on their way. "You two go on home and enjoy what's left of the evening."

"Are you sure? We could sit here and finish off the hot chocolate." Candie held up the thermos.

"Don't be silly. Nina, Porkchop, and I will enjoy the fire as it dies down. Hopefully I'll hear from Hank before too long." I bent and gave the pups another scratch between their ears. A sloppy kiss was my reward from the both of them.

Candie laughed as I wiped my slobber-covered hands on the legs of my jeans. "At least my Dixie doesn't leave a mess behind when she gives me some lovin'."

I stuck my tongue out at my cousin. Dixie was Candie's calico cat. She and Porkchop barely tolerated each other. Candie laughed, said, "Ta-ta," and waved her bejeweled fingers over her shoulder as she left my backyard snuggled up against Mark's side.

The little green monster raised its head as I thought about how Mark and Candie would spend the rest of their evening. Hopefully, tomorrow would be a better one for Hank and me.

CHAPTER THREE

I watched the embers of the fire die down for as long as I could before the night's chill forced me inside. "Come on, pups. Time for us to get out of this cold." I glanced at my watch. Two hours had passed since Hank left to collect his brother at The Dugout. I doubted he'd call at this late hour. I had hoped for at least a few loving words from him, even if they were over the phone. But maybe I was being selfish. After all, Hank did have his hands full dealing with Aaron.

Hank had laid down the law when Aaron came to live with him. First, he needed to get a job and do it on his own. Hank wasn't about to pull in any favors and ask our friends to employ Aaron. He had checked that off the list by answering Franny Goodway's ad in the *Tribune* for kitchen help. Since starting, Aaron had taken on more and more food prep responsibilities in Sweetie Pie's kitchen. He was from a large family and often had to fend for himself. As a result, he was pretty good in front of a stove.

Second, he had to stay sober. He'd managed to do that until tonight. When he lived in Albany, he ran with a pretty fast crowd whose main idea of having fun was spending the weekends getting drunk. Even when he was younger, there was always someone who could supply him with booze. His mom had had enough when he came home one night with a bloody nose and an eye swollen shut. She feared one of these nights Aaron's injuries might be more deadly. He had always looked up to his big brother, so she'd pleaded with Hank to take him in. Maybe Hank, being a detective for Wings Falls PD, would make an impression on Aaron and he'd straighten up. Hopefully, he'd cut all ties with the rough crowd he hung with before he moved north.

So much for my musings on Hank's brother. I was tired and imagined so were Nina and Porkchop. I clapped my hands to get their attention. "Come on, let's hit the sack." I tossed the sticks we'd been using to roast marshmallows into the fire pit and gathered up the leftover makings for our s'mores. Nina and Porkchop followed behind me with what was left of their rawhide bones clamped in their jaws. I nudged open the back door to my kitchen and walked over to the counter and deposited everything on it. I smiled and glanced around my kitchen. It was stuck in the 80s when my parents did their last makeover, but it held too many childhood memories for me to do a remodel like they do on those home improvement shows. That and also the lack of money it would take to do a "gut "job as all those homeowners proclaim needed to be done. Maybe with the release of my children's book, *Porkchop, the Wonder Dog,* starring my favorite dachshund, I could manage a few improvements.

Both dogs followed me into my living room. Next to my fireplace lay two fleece-covered doggie beds, pink for Nina and red plaid for Porkchop. I bought one for Nina when Hank became a more permanent part of Porkchop's and my lives. Nina would often accompany him on his visits to my home.

Nina snuggled into her bed while Porkchop climbed into his, scratched at the bottom to fluff up the filling, and then lay down.

A yawn escaped me. "Nighty, night," I called out to the two dogs as I walked down the hallway to my bedroom. I flipped on the light switch and stared at the empty bed that hugged the far wall. This certainly wasn't how I imagined this evening would end. Oh, well. Tomorrow was a big day, and I needed some sleep so I could handle all the activities awaiting me at the Taste of Wings Falls. I pulled on my not-so-flattering green, moose-decorated flannel pajamas and snuggled under my down comforter.

* * *

"Hank, come on, you can kiss better than that." I swatted at what I thought was Hank but was greeted with a tongue on my cheek. My eyes flew open. "*Umph.* Come on, you guys. It's barely…." I squinched my eyes to focus on the alarm clock sitting next to my bed. "Oh no, it's almost seven. No wonder you're up. Hungry, huh?" I turned to Nina. "I wonder why your daddy hasn't called yet." She cocked her head as if to say, *"Yeah, where is the big guy?"* My phone rang. Was this ESP? I flipped my phone open—and yes, I still had a flip phone. Even though there was a fancy new version of the flip phone, technology and I had a love-hate relationship, and the love part hadn't extended to my purchasing an iPhone, not yet at least. "Hey there, Hank. How did last night go?"

"Don't ask. I'll only say I'm not real happy with the baby bro right now."

"Okay, I won't ask, but are you okay?"

Nina must have heard her master's voice, as she inched up the bed and tried to nudge my phone.

"Nina misses you."

Hank's laughter came across the phone. Nina whined at the sound of his voice. "How about me? Do *you* miss me?"

"You know I do, but we've got to get moving. The pet parade is at nine o'clock. I have a costume Nina can wear." In fact, I had twelve to pick from. My publisher wanted a calendar featuring Porkchop to accompany the release of my book, so Nina and Porkchop had a number of costumes to pick from.

"All right, I'll stop at Sweetie Pie's and grab us some coffee and cider donuts to go."

I groaned. One of my favorite things about the fall season were cider donuts. I could eat a half dozen and not think a thing about it, except my yoga pants would be a tad snug. "You know how I love those donuts. Make sure you get enough to satisfy my craving for them."

"Never fear. I will. I'll see you in less than half an hour."

Porkchop and Nina tumbled in the sheets at the foot of my bed while I cradled my phone next to my ear. "Okay, I love you. Watch it, you, or you'll fall off the bed."

"What's all that noise I hear? Are you all right?"

"Yes, I'm fine. Porkchop and Nina are playing at the foot of my bed."

The playful dogs looked up at me at the mention of their names.

Hank's voice turned husky. "I really envy those pups. I'd like to be the one playing in the sheets with you right now."

Heat crawled up my neck at the thought of what Hank meant by "playing."

I cleared my throat. "Umm, hold that thought."

"I guess we'd better get this show on the road. I love you," he replied.

"I love you, too," I whispered back before I snapped my phone shut.

* * *

"What do you think? The pumpkin hat or the candy corn hat?" Hank and I sat on my den sofa sipping coffee and munching on the cider donuts he had brought with him. An array of costumes were spread out on the carpet at our feet. We'd tried all the costumes on the dogs and narrowed the choice down to a pumpkin-shaped hat or a candy corn-shaped one for Nina. Porkchop was easier to figure out. As soon as I pulled the cowboy hat with the sheriff's gold star on the front out of the plastic bin where I had stored it, he barked his approval.

Hank picked the pumpkin-shaped hat and placed it on Nina's head. "This one. It looks the cutest on her." He turned to Porkchop. "Sorry good buddy, but my Nina may give you a run for your money in her costume."

I jutted out my chin. "We'll see about that. Don't count on taking home the loving cup before you have it in your hands." I glanced down at Nina. "Or should I say paws? We'd better get going."

I gathered up our breakfast trash, took it into the kitchen, and shoved it into the garbage can. When I returned to the den, Hank had both dogs leashed up and the costumes in his hand.

"Let's get over to the park." I handed Hank his down vest then went to the coat closet in the living room to retrieve mine.

"Ready?" Hank asked. I took the dog's costumes from him so that Hank, always the gentleman, could open the front door for me. He brushed a kiss on my cheek as I passed by him.

* * *

The ride to Wings Falls Park was a short one from my house, less than ten minutes. Porkchop and I often took a walk to the park for exercise. This morning had been such fun trying the different costumes on the dogs that I hesitated to bring up last night's happenings with his brother, but I wanted Hank to know I cared about him and the problems he was having with Aaron. Maybe if he shared them with me, it would lighten his load. "How is Aaron? Did you find out what is bothering him?"

Hank's fingers tightened on the steering wheel of his Jeep. "Apparently, he and Franny's niece, Joy, are more involved than I thought. I guess they had an argument and it sent him over the edge. He's used to getting his own way, and Joy told him if they were going to continue with their relationship, he had to grow up and make something out of his life."

I turned towards him. Porkchop and Nina were settled in the back seat. "Wow, her ultimatum must have sent his head spinning."

Hank gave me a side-eyed look. "Yeah, he's always been able to wheedle what he wants from people. Especially with someone he cares about."

We pulled into a parking space next to the park and climbed out of the Jeep. Hank handed me Porkchop's leash. I scooped my pup up and placed him on the ground. Hank reached in for Nina. I grabbed Nina's pumpkin hat and the sheriff's hat for Porkchop and slipped them on their heads. They looked adorable as they walked next to us towards the park where the day's festivities would be held. They garnered *So cute*s and *Adorable*s as we walked past people gathered around the different craft and food booths set up in the park.

"Oh, look. Aaron and Joy appear to have made up." I pointed over to Sweetie Pie's booth. Aaron had his arm around Joy's slim waist as he stirred a pan of what I assumed was Franny's famous barbeque. Its aroma floated over to us and made my mouth water.

"Yes, it does, but Franny doesn't look very happy." Hank nodded his head towards Franny, who stood a few feet away from the booth. Franny and a gentleman, who I'd seen about town but didn't know personally, seemed to be engaged in a heated discussion. Her hands were balled into fists at her side, as if she were trying to restrain herself from giving him a good punch to his large nose.

CHAPTER FOUR

———

Porkchop lifted his long snout into the air, sniffing the same enticing aromas of barbeque pork I was. It didn't take much coaxing to lead him over to Sweetie Pie's booth.

I bent closer to the portable grill sitting on a folding table that was warming the shredded meat. "Hi, Aaron. Hi, Joy. I can't wait to taste one of Franny's famous barbeque sandwiches. My stomach is rumbling at the tantalizing scents coming from your grill."

A smile dimpled Joy's dark-skinned face. Like her Aunt Franny, her black, kinky hair was pulled back into a ponytail to comply with state health codes. Even though the afternoon was predicted to be in the mid-sixties, she wore a teal-colored sweatshirt to ward off the morning chill. A black half-apron was tied around her slim waist to keep the barbeque from staining her slim-fitting jeans. "Hi, Hank and Sam." She removed the plastic gloves covering her hands, reached down, and patted both Nina and Porkchop. "I'm sorry I don't have any doggie bones for you. We're only serving people food today."

Hank laughed as Porkchop and Nina turned their best sad eyes up to Joy. "I'm sure they're disappointed, but believe me, they won't starve."

I turned to Aaron and asked, "How are you this morning?" He blushed almost as red as the red plaid flannel shirt he wore. "I'm sorry to have interrupted your evening with Hank last night. Guess I was acting like a jerk."

"I'll second that," Hank said.

I tried to elbowed Hank in the ribs, but he was too well protected by the down vest he wore over a denim shirt, the same color as his crystal blue eyes. "Cut the kid a break. Young love doesn't always act rationally."

"He needs to grow up. He's not a teenager anymore," he whispered out of the side of his mouth.

"I hope you win the Best Barbeque Prize this year. You're up against some stiff competition with The Smiling Pig and The Round Up." I nodded towards the other two booths set up in the park a few yards from them.

"Yeah, Aunt Franny said The Round Up has won this competition for the last five years. But Aaron has tweaked our recipe, and I know it is a winner." Joy hooked her arm through Aaron's and gazed up at him with pride.

"You're a thief, and I'm going to let everyone in Wings Falls know it."

We all turned our heads at Franny's angry words. Porkchop and Nina growled.

"What's got Franny so upset with that fellow? In all the years I've known her, I've never heard her raise her voice with anyone. Who is he, anyway?" I asked, staring at Franny and a tall balding man sporting a paunch and in his mid-thirties if I guessed correctly.

A frown marred Joy's smooth forehead. "That's Edgar Jensen. He's the loan officer at the bank."

"He must be new to the bank. I haven't met him before, not that I've had to take out any loans lately." I was fortunate my egg-yolk yellow Volkswagen convertible Bug was paid for and I didn't have a mortgage on my house since my parents signed it over to me after I divorced my ex, George, five years ago. I had caught him doing the bump fuzzies with the secretary of the funeral home we co-owned together, The Do Drop Inn Funeral Parlor. My parents were tired of the cold and snowy upstate New York winters and moved to sunny Florida to enjoy evening cocktails on the lanai with their friends Marge and Herb Feinstein while watching the sun set.

"Excuse me. I need to see what's got Aunt Franny so upset." Joy turned towards her aunt.

Aaron placed a hand on Joy's arm. "Do you want me to come with?"

Joy shook her head. "No. Stay with the barbeque to make sure it doesn't burn. People will be lining up soon for a sandwich."

Aaron watched with a solemn look on his face as Joy walked over to her aunt and the man Franny was now shaking her finger at. A petite woman about five-foot-two, with shoulder-length, flaming red hair, joined the gentleman and spoke to him in a hushed voice. He turned an angry look on her and nudged her away from him.

Aaron turned down the flame on the burner and covered the barbeque with aluminum foil. "I don't like the looks of this. I'm going to see what's going on with that guy."

"Keep your cool," Hank called after him.

"Yeah, yeah." Aaron waved over his shoulder. He kicked dried leaves out of his way as he walked towards Joy.

I looked up at Hank. "I don't like the feel of this, either. Franny is the most even-tempered person I know. She would never lose her temper with anyone, even the most disgruntled customer in her restaurant."

Hank nodded. "I have to agree. Let's mosey on over and see what this is all about."

"Come on, Porkchop. We need to do a little sleuthing." I patted my leg for him to follow me.

Hank laughed. "I can't believe I'm encouraging you to butt your pretty little nose into something not concerning you. Let's go, Nina. I know you don't want to be left out of our investigating." Nina waddled alongside Porkchop as we walked over to the group.

"Edgar Jensen, you want to rob me blind. Are you pulling this scam on other customers at the bank?" Franny stood practically nose to nose with the fellow in question.

"So, what does this Mr. Jensen have to do with Franny?" I asked Aaron once we arrived at his side.

"From what I can gather, Franny has applied for a loan to help pay for Joy's tuition this year at Wings Falls Community College." Aaron squeezed Joy's hand. Tears rolled down her smooth cheeks.

A frown creased my forehead. "So, what is the big deal? People take loans out all the time to finance education."

Joy hiccupped and said, "I know, but Aunt Franny did this without my knowledge. She put Sweetie Pie's up as collateral. Now Mr. Jensen wants to add a 'special fee' on to the loan."

"Can he do that?" I frowned. Usually, loans were pretty cut and dry.

Joy shrugged her shoulders. "I don't know. Maybe. I guess so. With the economy so tight, I didn't make enough in tips this summer as I usually do. That's one of the reasons I decided to go to WFCC this year instead of returning home to Mercy College. The tuition there was twice as much, and Aunt Franny said she'd help me out and I could stay with her. I had no idea she was taking a loan out to help pay for my tuition."

I smiled. "The only reason?"

A blush colored Joy's cheeks as she looked up at Aaron. "Well, maybe not the *only* reason."

Aaron placed an arm around Joy's shoulder and pulled her to him. Joy snuggled her face into Aaron's flannel shirt.

Porkchop and Nina scratched the ground at Hank's feet. "Do you want me to step in, Joy, and try to diffuse the situation?" Hank asked.

Joy shook her head. Her curly ponytail bounced about her shoulders. "No, but maybe I should say something. This is all about me, anyway." Joy swiped at her tears and jutted out her chin as she walked towards her aunt. Aaron followed her.

My curiosity pulled me closer to Franny and this Edgar Jensen. Hank reached out a hand to stop me, but I kept on walking. I could hear him exhale a deep sigh as if he knew I was a woman on a mission—namely to eavesdrop. He was right behind me.

Joy looked at her aunt with pleading eyes. "Aunt Franny, I can wait another semester and work at Sweetie Pie's to save more money. You don't have to deal with this man."

The gentleman in question eyed Joy up and down with a lecherous glare. "Well, now what do we have here? You could certainly be the chocolate sauce on my sundae."

A collective gasp could be heard from all of us at Edgar's crude remark.

Aaron jumped between Franny and Edgar and shoved him, knocking him to the ground "Why you piece of slime. You're not fit to breathe the same air as she does," Aaron shouted, his fists clenched at his sides.

CHAPTER FIVE

———

Hank shoved Nina's leash at me and stepped to his brother's side. He placed a hand on his arm. "Aaron, back down. The last thing I want is to arrest you."

Aaron glared down at Edgar. "He's lucky we're not back in the hood. He'd be a dead man right now."

Joy stood next to me weeping. She pointed a shaking finger at Edgar Jensen. "This is all my fault. I should never have agreed to let Aunt Franny take out a loan from that man."

The petite woman with flaming red hair fell to the ground on her knees next to the man Aaron had shoved. "Are you the police? Arrest that man. He attacked my husband. He may have injured Edgar for life."

A crowd of gawkers was gathering around Franny's booth.

Franny pointed to the woman. "You do that, and I'll tell everyone who comes into my restaurant how your husband here made a pass at my niece." Franny tilted her head towards the man on the ground. "I'm sure it won't be good for Edgar's reputation at Wings Falls National Bank."

The woman's mouth gaped open like a goldfish seeking food. "Why, you wouldn't dare."

Franny placed her dark hands on her slim hips. "Try me."

Edgar pushed himself off the ground and looked around at the gathering crowd then at the woman who said she was his wife. He brushed off the leaves clinging to his pants. "Hush, Carol, you're making a mountain out of a mole hill. I may have just tripped over a tree root when the young man got too close to me. I guess a person can't give a young lady a compliment these days."

Hank stepped around Aaron. "Sir, I heard your compliment, and it was far from flattering. I'd say it bordered on sexual harassment."

Franny's black curls bobbed as she nodded her head in agreement. "You're right, Hank. And there are enough witnesses to what Mr. Jensen said to Joy to back it up. In fact, Mr. Jensen, I think you might want to rethink the extra 'special fee you want to tack on to my loan. I'm sure you wouldn't like the bank president, your father-in-law, to learn about what happened here today."

Edgar Jensen's face turned as red as the maple leaves fluttering down around us. "Are you threatening me?"

Franny's ponytail swayed back and forth as she shook her head. "Nope, only stating a fact."

Edgar's wife, Carol, tugged at his arm. "Come on dear. Let's take in the rest of the festival. You can talk business at the office on Monday if you have to." She led him towards a bench across the park from Franny's booth.

Joy ran a hand up and down Aaron's flannel shirt sleeve. "Are you all right? Thank you for coming to my defense. You are my knight in shining honor."

A smile replaced the fierce look on Aaron's handsome face. "Yeah, some knight I am. I could have killed that guy for what he said to you. And I may have jeopardized the loan your aunt was taking out for your education."

Franny tugged at her sweatshirt. Sweetie Pie's Café was printed across the front and back. "Now don't you go worrying about the loan. You'll go to WFCC this January and make your aunt proud. You're not going to waste those brains the good Lord gave you."

Joy pulled her aunt into a hug. "Aunt Franny, you are the best. What would I do without you?"

Franny looked over her shoulder at Aaron and smiled. "Oh, I think you'll be in pretty good hands.

"Show's over folks. Go and enjoy the rest of the festival." Hank motioned for the crowd gathered around Franny's booth to move along.

Heads bent to each other. People whispered and pointed at Aaron and Joy as they went on their way. I could only imagine what they were saying and how exaggerated this event would be by this evening.

I handed Nina's leash back to Hank. "I believe the pet costume parade will be starting soon. We should check in and make sure Nina and Porkchop are registered."

Hank nodded and turned to Aaron. "Can I trust you to remain cool headed and not do anything crazy while Sam and I are away? Between last night at The Dugout and today, you have two strikes against you."

Aaron gritted his teeth and turned his back to his brother. "I don't need a babysitter."

Hank heaved a deep sigh as we walked towards the sign-in table for the pet costume parade. "Sometimes I wonder if he does."

I looked up at his troubled face. "You're a great big brother. A lot of people would have thrown up their hands in disgust with their sibling by now, but not you. You love him a lot."

"Yeah, I do. Sometimes I see myself in him when I was younger."

I laughed. "Straight and narrow, by-the-book you were a problem child?"

Hank grinned. "You can't imagine what a hellion I was. If it wasn't for my dad, God rest his soul, I'd probably be behind bars right now."

I glanced at the booths we passed on our way to the pet costume parade check-in table. Already, people were crowded around booths set up to sell handmade jewelry, locally made maple syrup, hot sauce, lawn ornaments, and much more. A local author was even selling her bestselling mystery novel. Maybe next year I'd get a booth to sell my children's picture book, *Porkchop, the Wonder Dog*, due out in another month. "Tell me about your dad. Did you get your good looks from him?"

Hank gazed off into the distance as if lost in memories. "He was a tough task master. You had to tow the line around him, but he was a man grounded in a good moral fiber and love for his family and country. He was fresh out of high school when he volunteered to join the Army and serve in Vietnam."

I sucked in a breath. "It must have been hard on such a young man."

"Yeah, but his draft number was two, so he figured he might as well volunteer. He said it made him the man he was. Even though I gave him a hard time, he was my hero. After he left the Army, he became a firefighter. He was all about serving his country and then his community. When he passed away, his were big shoes to fill."

"What happened to him? He was rather young to die, wasn't he? Aaron must have been very small at the time."

"Yeah, he's the youngest of the seven of us, a little over one at the time. I was a teenager, already feeling my oats. There was a fire in a set of row homes in Albany. Dad went in to rescue a small child, and the roof collapsed on him. They discovered his body covering the child. She survived, but unfortunately, Dad didn't." Hank cleared his throat. Emotion filled those last words of his. I could tell he remembered losing his dad as if it were yesterday.

I reached over for his hand and gave it a little squeeze. Even though my parents lived way down in Florida and weren't a part of my daily life, I still called them every week. I couldn't imagine losing one of them. "You took over the role as man of the house?"

"Yeah, I guess I did. Someone had to help Mom keep all those kids in line, so the job fell to me. I'm not complaining. That's what you do for family."

My eyes welled up with pride at this man walking next to me. "You're a good man, Hank. I love you."

An angry voice drew my attention. "Look over there." I pointed to the bench where Edgar Jensen sat. Carol stood over him, shaking a finger at her husband. Gone was the concerned wife of a few minutes ago, replaced with a very angry one.

Hank turned towards where I was pointing. "Whoa, if looks could kill, Edgar would be a customer in your funeral home right now."

CHAPTER SIX

Porkchop started to bark. His leash tore out of my hand as he tugged on it. He might be small, but he was strong. He darted across the park with his leash slapping the ground behind him. The object of his attention, Hana, a beautiful Japanese Spitz, returned his barks. Porkchop and Hana became BFFs when Patsy Ikeda and I brought our dogs with us to our Monday morning hook-ins at our friend, Lucy Foster's, store, The Ewe and Me Woolery. Lucy supplied us hookers with the wool and patterns for our rug hooking habit. Porkchop and Hana had become The Ewe's shop dogs. They lay at our feet, quietly chewing on rawhide bones supplied by Lucy's husband, Ralph, while their mistresses hooked and gossiped.

Patsy was civil to me, but I thought she still harbored a few ill feelings since I accused her of murdering the owner of an animal shelter last year. Heck, it wasn't my fault she topped my suspect list because the guy blackmailed her. At the time, I topped another list, that of my grade school nemesis, Sergeant Joe Peters. Joe and I had a long history going all the way back to kindergarten. You see, at recess one day, Joe decided to use the playground's sandbox as his personal pee-potty. Well, I for sure wasn't going to play in pee-soaked sand, so I ratted him out to the teacher. Unfortunately, kids had long memories, and he was dubbed "Sandy" from that day forward. As payback, Joe, a member of the Wings Falls Police, along with Hank, placed me on the top of his suspect list for the murder of the shelter's owner.

Hana returned Porkchop's greeting and pulled on his leash to get to Porkchop. Patsy gave him the command to sit, and he immediately obeyed. I envied Patsy's control over her dog. I'd tried obedience classes with Porkchop, but to no avail. He had a mind of his own, along with Hank, and when on a mission like he was now, there was no dissuading him. Winded, I finally caught up with my pup, who was trying to persuade Hana to roll in the falling leaves with him.

"Hi, Patsy. Sorry about that. I guess Porkchop was excited to see Hana."

Patsy bent and stroked the long hair on her dog's back. A breeze fluttered the hair on his curled tail.

"No, problem. I was on my way to sign Hana in for the pet costume parade." Patsy held up a canvas bag in which I assumed was Hana's costume. "Porkchop looks adorable with his cowboy hat."

I laughed. "I think so, but I don't know if he'd agree with me."

Hank strode up and stood next to me. Nina sat at his feet, straining on her leash to join Porkchop in his leaf rolling. Hank nodded at Patsy. "Hi, Patsy. How are you doing? Great day for the Taste of Wings Falls."

"Yes, it is. I was on my way to sign Hana up for the pet costume parade. Then, I'll see what I can do to help out at the Loopy Ladies' booth. We were pretty successful last year in raising money for Camp Adirondack, and I hope we can top that total."

A wind whipped at the wool scarf I'd flung around my neck before I left home this morning. I made a grab for it before I had to chase it across the park. "Yes, we did." I turned to Hank. "We raised enough money to send three children from the city to the camp for a week."

Hank raised an eyebrow. "Wow, that is quite a bit. Who knew a bunch of hookers could be so productive with their wares?"

I poked Hank in the ribs. Patsy and I both laughed. "Hank, you know we're not *that* kind of hooker."

The raised voices from the bench occupied by Edgar and Carol Jensen caught our attention again. We all turned in their direction. Even our dogs stopped frolicking in the leaves and looked towards them.

Carol still stood with her hands on her hips and shaking her finger at Edgar as he sat on the bench. "Edgar, you fool. I need the money and now. You find a way to get it, or you'll be sorry." She stomped away from him towards the booth selling maple syrup.

I bent and rubbed the reddish-brown hair that stood up on Porkchop's back. In a soothing voice I said, "That's okay, buddy. Did those people upset you? I guess it's not all happy valley in the Jensen home."

Patsy bent and smoothed down Hana's fur, too. Apparently the raised voices had upset her dog. "The Wings Falls Senior Center sponsored a bus trip to the Saratoga Racino last week. I saw that woman there. Do you know her?"

Hank bent and scooped Nina up into his arms. I smiled as he petted her wrinkled head. She was his baby. She had started to whine when Carol raised her voice at Edgar. "That's Carol Jensen and her husband Edgar. He's the new loan officer at Wings Falls National Bank. From what I've heard, her dad is the president of the bank."

I was mulling over what Patsy said about Carol being at the Racino. Not that it was any big deal. I'd gone there a few times with Candie for a girl's night out. I set myself a budget of fifty dollars and played the quarter slots. Sometimes I won and sometimes I lost, but it was more about the fun I had trying to beat the machines and win the bazillion dollar jackpot. So far—no such luck. "How did she do at the Racino? Was she a winner?"

Patsy brushed at a strand of gray-streaked black hair the wind blew in her face. "Frankly, I don't know. When I saw her, she was at the bar ordering a drink. She didn't look unhappy, so I guess she was having a good night. Although, I didn't see him there." Patsy nodded towards Edgar, who sat on the park bench, staring down at his folded hands dangling between his knees.

I glanced at my watch. "Well, whatever marital problem they have is between them. We'd better get over to the sign-in table for the pups. The pet costume parade starts soon."

Hank placed Nina back on the ground, and then the three of us led our dogs over to the sign-in table. On our way, we had to dodge young kids dressed in costumes as they raced around the park. Batman and fairy princesses looked to be popular Halloween outfits this year.

Porkchop bounced up and down on his stubby legs with excitement as we approached the sign-in table. Nina and Hana were more reserved. Both wagged their tails and sniffed at the air filled with the scent of other animals.

Shirley Carrigan, who owned the For Pet's Sake Animal shelter, sat behind a folding table registering the various contestants. Shirley took over the shelter after her live-in boyfriend, Calvin Perkins, was murdered. Unfortunately, it was the first of three murders that I had been involved in either as a suspect or a sleuth. The only good thing was that was how I met Hank, over Calvin's dead body.

"Hi, Shirley. How are the signups going? From the looks of the crowd, I'd say there are more entrants than ever." I gazed around at the various pets dressed in their costumes.

Shirley pointed a pen at the crowd of pets gathered around the table. "You've got that right. Look at all the pets waiting for the parade to start."

I glanced at the pets ready to show off their costumes. The various costumes brought a smile to my face.

Nina growled at a dog of indeterminate breed dressed in a black cat outfit. Hank picked up Nina and whispered into his precious pup's ear, "That's okay, girl. The cat is only pretend." My Porkchop might put up with Candie's calico cat, Dixie, but Nina wasn't as tolerant.

Speaking of Candie and Dixie, I saw her rushing up to the sign-in table pushing a pet carriage. It resembled one of those folding strollers moms pushed their young children in. Candie came to an abrupt halt next to us. The ruffles on her purple sweater fluttered as she drew in a large breath of air. "Am I too late?"

"No, " I said and laughed. I pointed to the carriage. "Really?" I asked. I nodded at its occupant, Dixie. She sat curled up on a purple sequined pillow dressed as a fairy. Gauzy wings sprouted from her back, and a star-topped wand was attached to a front paw by a piece of elastic.

Candie jutted out her chin. "Yes, and my Fairy Queen here will win first prize, too. I understand Rob Anderson from the *Tribune* is going to take a picture of the winner and it will be on the front page."

Rob was a reporter for our local paper, the *Tribune.* He and I suffered each other's presence since his reporting had not always shown my friends or me in a favorable light.

"Where's Mark?" I asked.

Candie waved red-painted fingernails at me as she bent over the table to register Dixie. "He's busy at his table handing out campaign brochures. Even if he is running unopposed, he wants to meet with the people of Wings Falls face-to-face."

Mark's mayoral reelection was next month, and hopefully, he would serve another term as Wings Falls mayor.

Shirley stood up from her seat at the sign-in table and clapped her hands. "All right, folks. I think we have all the contestants registered for the pet costume parade." She held up a gold trophy. "One lucky pet will take home this beautiful trophy For Pet's Sake has donated, as the best costume in this year's contest. Also, he or she will have their picture taken by Rob Anderson here." She pointed to Rob. He held up his camera in a salute to us. "That lucky pet will have their picture on the front page of the *Tribune.*"

I let out a sigh. At least this time it wouldn't be me or someone I knew making the front page of the paper because of a murder. Fingers crossed it would be Porkchop.

CHAPTER SEVEN

———

"So, what do you think?"

I swiveled around to see Hana decked out in her costume. Patsy had kept it a secret until right before we were all lined up to parade before the judges.

"A pirate! How cute!" A black pirate's hat complete with a skull and crossbones printed on the front sat nestled amongst the long hair on Hana's head. A set of arms was attached to his outfit. One hand clutched a cutlass. Hana definitely looked like he was about to board a ship and sail the seven seas in search of pirate booty. I looked from Porkchop to Nina to Dixie and all the other pets lining up for the parade. My heart sank. It looked to me as if Hana would take home the trophy this year. Oh well. There was always next year. Anyway, the entrance fee went to a good cause, like all the other festivities today—Camp Adirondack.

"Okay, folks. Let's get this parade started." Shirley walked along the line of pets giving instructions on her way. She tapped a pen on the clipboard she carried.

Porkchop and I stood in front of Hank and Nina. Hank leaned over and whispered. "She could be a drill sergeant in the Army."

I giggled and swatted at his arm. "Be good. It's not easy wrangling up all of these animals so they can parade around the park and past the judges."

Candie stood in front of me rocking Dixie back and forth in her stroller, hoping the motion would keep her calm. "Do you know who any of the judges are? I heard Father Pete was going to be one. I wonder when I pass by him and mention I'd throw in an extra twenty at Mass tomorrow if he'd vote for Dixie."

My mouth fell open. "Candie, are you suggesting you can bribe Father Pete?" Father Pete was the priest at Saint Anthony's

Catholic Church where Candie and I attended Mass on Sunday mornings.

Candie's eyebrows rose. Her Passion Pink lips formed an O. "Me? Why, I'd never do such a thing."

"Let the parade begin," shouted Shirley.

Dogs barked and strained at their leashes as their masters and mistresses fought to keep them under control. Cats also had to be leashed or, as in Dixie's case, confined to a pet stroller.

After about twenty minutes of strutting their stuff, the pets arrived back at the starting point. There were only two minor incidents. A chihuahua wearing a sombrero broke loose from its master and darted across the park chasing a squirrel, and a boxer wearing a Frankenstein costume sat down and refused to budge so the line had to detour around him. Apparently, he'd had enough of parading around as Frankie.

Hank, Candie, and I stood together near the sign-in table. "So, who do you think is going to win?" I asked as I rubbed my hands together to warm them. Clouds had covered the sun, causing the temperature to drop.

"I'd say there is some stiff competition this year," Hank said. Nina sat obediently at his feet.

Candie pulled her sweater closer to her body. A wind had picked up, rustling the leaves on the trees throughout the park. "That there is. But I think my Dixie is the cutest kitty here, no matter what any ol' judge says."

I shook my head and laughed. Father Pete walked up to Shirley and handed her a piece of paper. As he walked past us, he bent and patted Porkchop. He looked up and said, "Nice cowboy hat," then strode off.

I turned to Hank. "See? I told you Porkchop's costume is a winner."

"We'll see," Hank replied.

Shirley waved the piece of paper in the air. "Folks. If I can have your attention. The votes are in, and here are the winners of this year's Taste of Wings Falls Pet Costume Contest. Second place and runner-up, Dixie Hogan, owner, Candie Parker-Hogan."

I clapped my hands and squealed. Porkchop barked at all the excitement. I handed his leash to Hank and threw my arms around my cousin. "Congratulations."

"Yeah," she mumbled into my ear. "She should have won first place."

"Oh, don't be such a sour puss. Look at all the contestants Dixie beat out." I spread my hands to take in the crowd standing near us.

"I guess you're right." Candie plastered on a smile and walked up to Shirley to accept a smaller version of the gold plastic trophy that would be awarded to the first-place winner.

I picked Porkchop up and cuddled him close to me. "Okay, Porkie, get ready to take the trophy home. I have the perfect place for it on our living room fireplace mantel."

Shirley cleared her throat. "Ta-dah. And now for this year's first place winner—Hana Ikeda and his pirate costume."

Patsy's hand flew to her chest. She bent and wrapped her arms around Hana's neck in a hug then walked up to the table to accept the trophy from Shirley.

My mouth dropped open. "What? But Father Pete said your costume was cute, Porkchop."

Hank put an arm around my shoulder. "It is cute, but it doesn't mean he thought it was a winner."

"*Humph.*" I wasn't in the mood for Hank's words of wisdom. I wanted to wallow in my self-pity a little longer since I still thought Porkchop and I were cheated out of the trophy.

Rob Anderson stepped to the front of the table, a camera clenched in his hand. "Can I have both winners over here." He pointed to an area next to the table.

"Go on." I nudged Candie's arm.

Candie hurried forward. "Oh, Dixie is going to be in the paper, too. How exciting! She really is a star."

After Rob snapped Dixie's photo, Candie took her place next to us. "I need to get back to Mark's table and help him hand out campaign flyers."

"Okay," I said and gave her a hug before she walked away to join her husband.

"Congratulations," I called out to Patsy as she led Hana up to have his picture taken.

A familiar voice caught my attention. I looked over to see Joe Peters pointing a finger in Edgar Jensen's face. Anger filled Joe's voice. "We need that loan, and we need it now. You have no right to hold it up. Our credit is stellar."

I looked up at Hank. "Woah. Joe looks like he could haul off and slug Edgar. What's he so angry about?"

Hank shook his head. That lock of brown hair that had a mind of its own fell over his forehead. I reached up and pushed it back. "The other day at the station, he mentioned his wife wants to open up a consignment shop here in town and they applied for a loan at the bank. He said he put up his house as collateral."

"Wow. That's taking a big risk. Especially since a good number of businesses go bust within the first five years after opening."

Hank shook his head as we walked away from the pet parade table. "Yeah, but I guess things haven't been hearts and flowers between him and Portia lately. He said she's going through some kind of mid-life crisis, especially since their last kid just went off to college. She doesn't feel as if she has a purpose in life anymore, and opening this store would give her a reason to get up in the morning."

I placed Porkchop on the ground and rolled my eyes. "I'm sorry, but I don't have much sympathy for her. That woman's main purpose when we were in school together was to make my life miserable."

"How so?"

"Miss Perky Portia was the head cheerleader in high school and thought I and all the other bookworms were fair game for her snide remarks," I said, remembering all the times I hid in the girl's bathroom to avoid passing her in the school's halls.

Hank drew me to his side again and kissed the top of my curly-haired head. "Well, it looks like you came out the winner in the end. Or…let me phrase it this way. I got the first-place prize."

I leaned up and kissed him. "I feel the same way."

Hank was breathing heavy after our kiss.

I glanced over to where Joe Peters stood. He was still pointing a finger at Edgar Jensen and arguing. "I hope he doesn't do anything foolish to make his wife happy."

CHAPTER EIGHT

———

"But that's Sandy's problem and not mine. I'd better check in at the Loopy Ladies' booth," I said, using Joe's childhood nickname and banishing any thoughts of Portia from my mind.

Hank frowned and shook his head. "Okay, I should probably make sure Aaron is behaving. You'd think at twenty-one he'd have a little more sense. Do you want me to take Porkchop with me?" Hank held his hand out for Porkie's leash.

"No. He'll be fine. He's used to all the Loopy Ladies since I take him with me on Monday mornings when we all meet to hook at The Ewe and Me. Don't be too hard on Aaron. After all, he didn't have your dad's influence like you." I leaned over and gave Hank another kiss then bent and patted Nina.

"Okay, Mother," he replied.

I laughed. "I'll take that as a compliment. The few times I've met your mom, I thought she was really nice."

"Yeah, she is. One of the best."

I thought about my parents and how lucky I was to have them.

"Stop by the Loopy Ladies' booth when you're finished with your big brother duties." I gave Hank one last kiss then headed over to the Loopy Ladies' booth with Porkchop in tow.

A crowd was already gathered around our booth, fingering the various mug rugs spread across the table and admiring the small, hooked rugs hanging from the sides of the booth.

Gladys, Marybeth Higgins, and Helen Garber sat on folding chairs behind the table.

"Hi, ladies. Are we making any money?" I asked as Marybeth took payment for a small rug featuring a crow with a cherry dangling from its beak.

Gladys nodded her orange-dyed, corkscrew curl–topped head. She dyed her hair to correspond to the season or holiday. In fact, she had even dyed her hair purple when Candie and Mark got married to match the color scheme of their wedding, violet. Gladys drew out a wad of bills from the fanny pack fastened over her fleece jacket. "It's only a little after eleven, and look at the haul we've made."

"Phew, what is that awful smell?" Helen Garber waved a gloved hand in front of her nose.

I had to admit this time Helen's complaint was justified. Along with the money came a pungent smell out of Gladys's fanny pack.

Gladys jutted out her chin. "I made myself half a ham sandwich with limburger cheese in case I got hungry."

Helen pointed at the wad of bills Gladys clutched in her gnarled fingers. "You old bird. What will the bank teller say when we hand them that smelly money?"

Gladys's thin lips drew down into a frown as she started to rise out of her chair. "Who are you calling an old bird? Why, my brain is sharper than yours any day of the week."

Helen stood and tugged at the hem of her lime-green sweater.

Oh, dear. Were these two women going to come to blows? I clapped my hands. "Wonderful. Porkchop and I are here to help if you want to walk around the park and take in all the vendors."

"We're all right for now." Gladys turned to Marybeth.

"Maybe I'll take a potty break. My morning coffee is calling." Marybeth, who had finished with the customer, had sat quietly during Helen and Gladys's tiff. She edged out of her chair and walked around to the front of the booth.

"When you come back, I think I'll stretch my legs a little," Gladys said.

I strolled around the table and sat in the chair Marybeth had vacated. Porkchop edged under the table and stood at Gladys's feet. I wondered if he wanted a bite of Gladys's sandwich.

Gladys bent and scratched Porkchop with her gnarled hand. "How's my favorite wiener dog doing? You look adorable in your cowboy hat. I gather by the star on the front you are the new sheriff in town. Did you bring home the trophy?"

I shook my head. "No, the honor went to Hana."

Glady cradled Porkchop's head in her hands. Porkchop gazed up at her with his chocolate-brown eyes. "Ah, but look at his sweet face. How could those judges vote for anyone but him? You were robbed, Porkchop."

"I'd agree with you, but Father Pete was one of the judges, so I'm going to assume all was above board with the judging."

Porkchop leaned farther into Gladys's hands as she scratched his back. He was definitely enjoying the attention. "I guess if you can't trust a man of the cloth, who can you?"

I dug a rawhide bone out of my tan and brown Coach purse. Designer purses were a weakness of mine. The bone would keep him occupied while I helped man the booth. "It looks like the Loopy Ladies had a great morning so far. Wonderful. You missed the excitement at Franny's booth, though."

Gladys arched one of her gray eyebrows. "Drat. What did I miss?" She loved to keep up on the town's gossip. Usually by listening to the police scanner she had turned on day and night.

I relayed to her what took place earlier in the day with Franny and Edgar Jensen. I didn't leave out the tidbit about Aaron pushing Edgar, but I omitted Aaron's threat towards him. I believed he'd only said it in the heat if the moment. No need to have people think he was capable of murder.

Glady's orange curls bobbled as she nodded her head. "Good for Aaron, sticking up for Joy. Hank should be proud of his brother. This Edgar fellow sounds like a real creep."

"Gladys! Hank can't condone violence. Even if the guy did deserve a poke in his big belly."

The mug rugs bounced when Gladys slapped the top of the table. "You're darn tootin' he did. If anyone talked to me that way, my Pookie Bear would have knocked him flat on his keester." Pookie Bear was Frank Gilbert, Gladys's live-in boyfriend. "It's funny you should mention this Edgar fellow. While we were sitting here, between customers, Marybeth mentioned her brother, Clint, was dealing with a person at the bank for a loan to get a new stove and refrigerator he needs for his restaurant."

Clint Higgins owned the newest barbeque joint in Wings Falls, The Smiling Pig. He'd opened it earlier this year, and it was an instant success. Hank and I had eaten there a number of times and could attest to why it was. "So, what did she say about the loan?"

Gladys looked to the right then the left. She leaned in closer to me. "Well, it seems Clint spent everything he had renovating his restaurant before he opened up and didn't have the money to buy a new stove and refrigerator. He was hoping they would last at least until his restaurant was on firmer ground."

I blew out the breath I didn't know I was holding. "Wow, those are expensive items. I can't imagine what a restaurant-grade refrigerator and stove would cost. I see what a regular one goes for at the local home improvement stores, and it blows my mind." I'd have to keep praying my Coppertone fridge would hang in there until *Porkchop, the Wonder Dog* was a resounding success. Maybe then I would be able to afford a new one.

"You can bet your sweet patootie they cost a bundle. Clint's been dealing with this Edgar fellow at the bank, but he's making Clint put the restaurant up for collateral, and Marybeth mentioned something about him charging high interest rates, too, like some kind of 'special fee.' I didn't understand what it was all about," Gladys continued.

So, Edgar was charging Clint a "special fee", too? Was this all above board or did he think that because his father-in-law was president of the bank, he could get away with something shady? Would people stand for this without there being any repercussions?

Gladys pointed over my shoulder. "Oh, lookee. Here comes Candie. What's she pushing in that adorable carriage?"

I turned to look where Gladys's gnarled finger was pointing. Candie walked across the park towards us with Dixie sitting like a queen in her stroller, the trophy she'd won nestled next to her.

"Hey, ladies. How's things going?"

Gladys rose from her seat and walked around to see Dixie. "A fairy princess, I presume?" Gladys touched one of Dixie's gossamer wings then reached over to lift the trophy out of the stroller.

Dixie hissed and swatted at Gladys's hand.

"Whoa." She snatched her hand out of the way of Dixie's claws.

Candie stroked the top of her cat's head then pointed to her cat. "Dixie, now you behave. That wasn't very nice of you. I'm sorry, Gladys. Dixie has developed quite an attitude since she won her trophy. I don't know where she gets it from."

I coughed. Luckily, I wasn't drinking anything, or I'd have choked. "You don't know where your cat gets her attitude? You know what Memaw Parker used to say… 'When you point your finger at someone, there are three pointing back at you.' Take a look at where those three fingers of yours are pointing."

Candie stuck her tongue out at me.

I shook my head at my cousin's antics. "Is Mark still at his booth?"

"Yes, he's, you know… Handing out *Vote for Mark Hogan* brochures and bumper stickers, answering any questions his constituents may have. He doesn't need me cramping his space. He can hold down his table by himself, so I thought I'd stroll over and see how things are going here."

I wondered if Candie was still sensitive about the racy pictures of her and an ex-fiancé that were published in the town's newspaper a few months ago. She'd feared she had ruined Mark's chances of reelection, but he'd won the primary in a landslide. I gave her hand a squeeze to let her know she shouldn't worry. Mark and his reelection campaign would be fine.

"Gladys said it's been a great morning so far." I motioned to the empty spaces on the walls of the tent where rugs had hung earlier.

Candie clapped her hands. "That's fabulous."

"Yes, and Sam has been filling me in on the latest gossip about that scoundrel Edgar Jensen." Gladys's gray eyes twinkled with excitement at the latest gossip.

Candie looked at me. I hadn't had the time to tell her what had happened at Franny's booth earlier. I relayed to her what took place and Marybeth's account of her brother's dealings with Edgar.

"You know, Mark mentioned Edgar while I was sitting with him. Bill Collins from The Round Up has applied at City Hall for permits to do work on his restaurant. He stopped in Mark's office, complaining about this Mr. Jensen and what he had to go through to get a loan from the bank. Mark said he was pretty angry. Spitting mad is what he said. He was afraid Bill would burst a blood vessel when he was talking about Edgar."

CHAPTER NINE

"Hi, ladies. Sam, can you take a break so we can go sample some of the fabulous barbeque offered here at the Taste today?" Hank stood on the other side of the table. Nina and her precious wrinkled body stood next to him. Nina's wrinkles were the only ones I would label as cute. In my midfifties, I was applying nightly lotion to ward mine off.

I glanced at my watch. Twelve o'clock. It had been an interesting, if not exasperating, hour with Helen and Gladys squabbling about everything from the prices the Loopy Ladies should charge to how the rugs should be displayed. To me, the prices were fair and the arrangement of the rugs was great. I mean, how many ways could you display a coaster or small rug? But what did I know, right? Their bickering started to give me a headache, and I was sure Porkchop, too. I rose from my folding chair and walked around the table to stand next to Hank. I reached up and kissed his stubbled cheek. His whiskers prickled my lips but in a wonderful way. They shot a thrill down to my toes.

Helen's head turned to Hank and me. She patted her hairspray-lacquered, red-dyed French twist. The buttons on her lime-green sweater strained as she thrust out her chest. Helen, if nothing else, had a love for color—the louder the better. She gazed up at Hank and batted her eyelashes. "Why hello, handsome."

In your dreams, I thought as I slipped my arm possessively through Hank's. At that moment, my stomach growled.

Hank laughed. "I guess that answers my question. Let's head on over to the food booths and grab some barbeque. I don't know if I'll be able to judge who has the best. From the aromas floating around the park, they all smell great."

I agreed with Hank. We'd eaten at all three of the restaurants vying for first place and were never disappointed by what we were served. "Ladies, will you be okay if I leave now?"

"We'll be fine," they both answered in unison.

I laughed as we walked away. Gladys and Helen continued their "discussion" about displaying the Loopy Ladies' wares. Porkchop and Nina trotted along beside us. Both of them stopped every few feet and sniffed the ground in hopes of any goodies the fairgoers may have dropped. "Don't worry, Porkchop. Momma tucked some kibble in my purse before we left home for you and Nina to munch on while we humans fill our tummies with barbeque.

"Which restaurant do you want to sample first?" Hank asked as we approached the food tents.

My nose twitched at the mouthwatering aromas. I pointed to The Round Up's booth. "We're here, so we might as well indulge. The line doesn't look like it's going to get any shorter." I scanned the area, and a long line of people snaked around all the food booths. People stood two deep, chatting and, like Hank and me, anticipating a great taste bud experience at all three booths.

Chris and David Collins, the sons of the owner, Bill Collins, manned the stainless steel warmers holding their prize-winning barbeque. Bill, dressed in jeans, a western-style shirt with pearl snap buttons, and wearing his signature Stetson, stood next to his apron-clad sons, chatting up his customers. "Make sure you vote for The Round Up's barbeque. You won't taste any better here today. I guarantee."

Finally, Hank and I stepped up for our serving. I thought my taste buds were going to shrivel up and die if they had to wait any longer. The aroma of the barbeque had had my mouth watering for the last five minutes.

"Hello, Miss Sam and Detective. Ready for your toes to curl at the taste of my delicious barbeque?" Bill asked, pointing to the warmers sitting on the table next to him.

Hank held out his hand for the paper plate filled with a barbeque sandwich and potato chips Bill's sons were serving up. "We sure are. Sam and I have enjoyed your fine cooking before and have never been disappointed."

Hank gave the plate to me. David Collins, the younger of Bill's sons, scooped out another helping of barbeque and placed it on a bun then handed it to Hank.

"Hank's right. We've never been disappointed." I thought I'd faint if I didn't sink my teeth into this delicious-smelling sandwich soon.

"I hope we can still keep serving up my grandad's recipe," David said. Unlike his short and stocky father, he was tall and thin with long brown hair he pulled back into a ponytail. A diamond earring winked from his left ear. Chris, his older brother, was tall like him but wore his hair in a buzz cut. Both brothers had followed in their dad's footsteps and worked at The Round Up. It was rumored that Bill was looking towards retirement and was about to hand the restaurant over to his sons to carry on the family tradition.

My eyebrows rose in question. What had David meant by his remark? Were either he or his brother thinking of leaving the family business? I didn't think this would settle very well with Bill. The Round Up had been in the family since the 50s. I believed barbeque sauce flowed in Bill's veins.

I scanned the food tent area for an empty picnic table so Hank and I could enjoy our meal. Most of the tables were full of other people enjoying their meals. I spotted an empty one under a maple tree, whose red leaves floated down whenever a breeze stirred its limbs.

I placed my plate on the picnic table and brushed fallen leaves off the wooden bench. Hank did the same, and then we sat next to each other. I reached into my purse and pulled out the plastic bag of kibble I'd placed in there this morning before I left the house. I had also tucked a bottle of water and a folding dog bowl in there. "Here you go, pups," I said as I shook the kibble into my hand and offered nuggets to each dog. Next, I unscrewed the top of the water bottle and poured some into the folding water bowl.

Hank leaned over and kissed me on the cheek. "Thanks."

"For what?" I asked.

He pointed to Nina, who sat gobbling down the kibble I had placed before her. "For taking care of my princess."

I laughed. "Of course. I would always take care of Porkchop's BFF."

Hank grinned. "Sam, you do a great job of that and her owner."

Heat crawled up my neck. "Come on. Let's enjoy our sandwiches."

I took a bite of my pulled pork and silently groaned at the heavenly flavor teasing my taste buds.

I reached for the napkin Bill Collins had handed us before we left their booth and wiped my lips. Eating barbeque was not for the overly tidy eater. "So, how is it?"

Hank swallowed. "Just as good as I remember from the last time we ate at The Round Up. What do you think David meant when he mentioned he hoped to be able to keep serving his grandfather's recipe? Has something happened that The Round Up might close? I thought Bill's sons were next in line to run it. They always seem happy whenever we stop in there."

I looked down to see what Porkchop and Nina were doing under the picnic table. They lay snuggled up next to each other, snoozing. The morning's event must have worn them out. I smiled then turned to Hank. "Earlier, when I was helping out at the Loopy Ladies' booth, Candie mentioned Bill had stopped by Mark's office at city hall."

Hank swallowed a mouthful of barbeque. "What does that have to do with The Round Up?"

"Well, it seems someone reported The Round Up for building code violations. They have to make some improvements or be shut down."

"Hasn't The Round Up been in business since the 50s?" Hank asked.

"Yes, it has. It was started by Bill's father and has been a fixture of Wings Falls ever since. But I guess someone reported them, and the Department of Health turned up one day and wrote them up for some violations. Bill apparently went to the bank and applied for a loan to make the improvements and got in a heated argument with the loan officer."

Hank pushed his plate away from him. "Let me take a guess—Edgar Jensen."

CHAPTER TEN

———

Clouds floated in front of the sun. A chill wind rustled the leaves in the maple tree above us. Red and yellow leaves floated down onto our table. I rubbed my hands together. I wished I had a mug of hot coffee to wrap my fingers around. Porkchop shifted his body across my feet. I welcomed the warmth that radiated from him. "Yep. Candie said Bill went into a real rant in Mark's office. He told Mark he felt like strangling Edgar. Mark made him sit for a while until he calmed down."

"For someone who's only been in town six months, this Edgar sure has ruffled a few feathers. How does he keep his job at the bank?"

I couldn't agree with Hank more. "Apparently, his father-in-law is the president of the bank."

Hank swiped a napkin across his mouth. "Ahh, I guess that explains a few things. So, we have Franny Goodway applying for a loan to help her niece with college expenses. Clint Higgins needs a new stove and refrigerator. Bill Collins has the health department breathing down his neck. And let's not forget Joe Peters. His wife Portia wants to open up a clothing store in Wings Falls. That's quite a list of people who have a beef with Jensen."

I blinked. Hank left off one other possible person from his list who wasn't fond of Edgar Jensen—his brother Aaron. Was it intentional or a slip of his memory?

"Hey, peeps, why so serious?"

I turned to see Candie and her new hubby, Mark, standing behind us. "Hi yourself. What are you two up to? And where's Dixie?"

Candie clutched on to Mark's arm. "All the hubbub and people were unsettling to my sweetums, so I ran her home."

Hank and I rose from the table and gathered our paper plates. Hank, being the gentleman he was, took mine from me and deposited them into the nearest trash can.

Candie pointed to Hank and leaned in close to me. "He has such good manners. Memaw Parker would have loved him."

"Yes, she would have, like she would have adored Mark, too."

A grin spread across Candie's face. "Yes, she would have adored my sugar, here." Candie squeezed Mark's arm.

"What are you ladies whispering about?" Mark asked.

"Girl talk, sugar. Just girl talk."

Adults and children alike stood crowded around the various booths lining the sidewalks snaking through Wings Falls Park. Many of the children running through the park were dressed in their Halloween costumes. They carried bags and small buckets to hold the candy various vendors handed out. I loved the excitement generated by the Taste. Wings Falls was a wonderful place to live and raise a family. Unfortunately, my ex George and I were never blessed with children, and being in my midfifties, baby carriage days had passed me by. I shook my head to dispel these unsettling thoughts. That was the past, and now I had a wonderful man in my life who loved me. I reached for Hank's hand and gave it a squeeze. He looked down at me and smiled.

He squeezed my hand. "Everything all right?"

I returned his smile. "Yep, perfect."

"Hi, Jane," I called out as we walked past a Wings Falls fire engine. Jane Burrows, a fellow Loopy Lady and the town's head librarian, stood next to the large engine and her boyfriend Jim Turner, the Wings Falls fire chief. The fire engine was decked out in orange pumpkin–shaped lights. Jane and Jim both held a bucket full of candy and were handing it out to children. Laughing kids were allowed to climb into the driver's seat of the fire truck. I imagine visions of someday driving one floated through their heads.

"Hi Aunt Sam."

There were only two boys who called me by that name. I looked up at the cab of the fire engine, and there sat Harry and Larry, my ex's twin boys. Their mother, Anna, and father stood on the opposite side of the truck. I groaned. While I loved the boys, I could have done without seeing their parents. George and I tolerated each other only because we were business partners in the Do Drop Inn

Funeral Parlor. I was more of a silent partner since I had footed the bill to purchase the Do Drop when we were first married. But Anna, I was civil to her only because it was how I was raised. Years of following Memaw Parker's rules of etiquette were ingrained in me.

"Boys, get down from there now, before you break something," Anna admonished the boys.

"Aw, Mom," the towheaded boys said in unison.

Harry and Larry scrambled down from the truck and ran over to me. "I want to be a fireman when I grow up," Harry said, bouncing from one foot to the other in his fireman's costume.

"Me, too," Larry said in a matching outfit.

I laughed. "Well, I'd say you two are dressed for it. Wouldn't you agree, Jim?"

Jim ruffled Harry's blond hair. "We always need good firemen, and I think you two boys would make fine recruits."

Larry squinched up his five-year-old face. "What's a recruit?"

Jim bent down to the boy's eye level. "It's a person who is in training to be a fireman. Here, let me see your muscle so I can tell if you are strong enough to pull the firehoses."

Both boys bent their arms in an attempt to flex their muscles. Jim gave them a gentle squeeze then straightened up. "What do you think, Detective Hank and Mayor Mark?"

Hank turned to Mark. "I believe they would make fine firemen when they grow up. What do you say, Mayor Mark?"

"I certainly agree with you, Detective. Wings Falls would be proud to have them on their fire fighting force," Mark said, nodding.

The boys jumped with glee. "Mom, Dad, did you hear what Detective Hank and Mayor Mark said?"

Anna and George had walked around the fire engine and joined their sons. Anna glared at me. She saw me as a threat to her and George. Yeah, right, like I'd ever want the two-timing cheater back. "I heard them. You guys can be whatever you want to be when you grow up. Now let's move along. There's lots more to see."

"Before you guys leave, I would like to make you Junior Fire Marshalls." Jim reached into his bucket and handed Harry and Larry plastic Junior Fire Marshall badges.

A million-dollar grin spread across both boys' faces. Their smiles warmed me down to my cold tootsies.

"Wow, look at these, Mom and Dad. We're Junior Fire Marshalls." Both boys cradled the plastic badges in their hands as if they were rare treasures. Which I guess they were to these two youngsters.

"Thanks, Jim," George said. He had been quiet until now. "You look really nice today, Sam."

Ugh. I rolled my eyes. Couldn't George just move on and enjoy his family? I know he and Anna were having some issues, but paying me a compliment wasn't going to help, especially since she thought George still had the hots for me. Nope. Never. Not going to happen.

Anna grabbed George's arm and yanked him away from the firetruck. "Come on, George. I'm hungry for a taste of barbeque." As they moved away, I heard Anna scolding George for talking to me.

Hank frowned at the retreating couple. He placed an arm around my shoulder and tugged me close to his side. "When is the guy going to learn we're a couple? And he has no rights to you."

We said our goodbyes to Jane and Jim and walked towards the flatbed holding Farmer Dickenson's large pumpkin. Porkchop pulled at his leash and started to bark. The reddish-brown hairs on his back stood on end. "What's the matter, Porkie? It's only a big pumpkin." I bent and tried to smooth down his fur, with no success. He still growled and tugged at his leash.

Candie pointed to the pumpkin. "That certainly is a big one, isn't it, Porkie, baby? It must be a little scary to a little fellow like you."

Mark walked over to the flatbed. "Scooter Dickenson told me it weighed over two thousand pounds."

"Phew wee, that sure is a whole lot of pumpkin pies," Candie said.

Hank joined Mark at the truck. He placed his hand on the pumpkin and gave it a little push. It wobbled under his hand. "I'll have to tell Scooter to secure it a little better. I'm afraid of it rolling off onto the ground."

CHAPTER ELEVEN

———

As we walked about the park, I stopped to admire the wares of a number of the vendors. "Wait one minute. That's Montana Casey's booth. I love her essential oil perfumes." I tugged Hank to a stop before a table covered with a dark green satin cloth. Resting on top were small bottles of Montana's fabulous natural oil products—bars of soap, skin lotions, shampoos and, my favorite, perfumes. There was sandalwood, peppermint, rose, lemon, jasmine, and many more. Each had a specific natural benefit to it. My favorite—her lavender-scented perfume. I found the perfume was very calming. I only had to open the vial, take a sniff, and I felt the day's tensions melt away. I swear it also helped reduce my headaches, especially when I had to deal with George and his whining about the Do Drop or how Anna didn't understand him, for which he got no sympathy from me.

"Hi Montana. How's the day been going for you?" I glanced around at the people gathered at her booth. "You look like you've been pretty busy. I need another bottle of your lavender perfume." I dug into my Coach bag for my wallet.

Montana was a tall slender woman in her midthirties. Long brown hair flowed down her back from beneath a blue and gray–striped knit hat cap pulled on her head. She smiled at Hank and me. "It's been crazy busy. But I'm not complaining. I'm happy to share my knowledge of the benefits of my products with people." She reached for the bottle of lavender I held in my hand and started to place it in a bag.

I shook my head. "No use wasting a bag. I'll tuck it into my purse." I handed over the money I owed her.

"Thanks, Sam. I appreciate your business."

"Heck, this little bottle has calmed my nerves on more than one occasion." I waved to Montana then reached for Hank's hand.

He gave it a gentle squeeze. "That stuff really work?" He nodded towards my purse.

"It works for me. Especially when I have to deal with George."

"Maybe I should get a few cases of it and see if it helps with Aaron."

I laughed. "Oh, come on. He can't be that bad."

Hank shook his head. "No, I guess it could be worse. At least he's not a murderer."

"Oh, look, there's Mark and Candie."

"I wondered what happened to y'all." Candie was snuggled up against Mark, her arm slipped through his.

"We stopped at Montana's booth on the way over. I needed a bottle of her lavender perfume. I'm running low."

Candie held up a small bag she clutched in her hand. "I'm surprised I didn't see you there. I bought a bar of her soap. Nothing touches my skin but her rose geranium–scented soap. It smells delicious. Right, sugar?" Candie gazed up at Mark. A blush tinted his cheeks.

I agreed. She did have porcelain smooth skin.

We came to a booth where six plastic pumpkins were stacked on top of each other to form a pyramid. For two dollars, you were given a ball and had three chances to topple the pumpkins. Frank Gilbert or, as Gladys referred to him, Pookie Bear, stood behind the table juggling two balls in his hands. He was Gladys's boyfriend. She had once informed me he did a great job keeping her tootsies warm on a cold winter's night. All of which I thought was TMI. "Hi folks. Ready for some fun? Fellas, for two dollars, you could win one of these great prizes for your sweetie. It's for the benefit of Camp Adirondack." He pointed to an assortment of stuffed animals lining the counter behind him.

"Hi Frank. I see both you and Gladys are busy at the fair this year." I nodded in the direction of the Loopy Ladies' booth.

"Yeah, she wrangled me into manning this booth while she's busy with your Loopy Ladies' booth, but I don't mind. It's for a good cause."

"Hank," I said, "see if you can win a teddy bear for me."

Frank reached out and took the two dollars Hank held out to him.

Hank handed me Nina's leash. Porkchop's and Nina's noses were busy sniffing the ground at our feet for any dropped cider doughnuts, popcorn, or other goodie a fairgoer might have left for their doggie dining pleasure.

Hank took the balls from Frank. "Let me see if I still have my high school pitching arm and win you a bear." He took aim and threw the balls at the pumpkins but failed to knock all of them down. He turned to me and shrugged. "Sorry, Sam. Guess I'm not the star player I once was."

I reached up and planted a kiss on his cheek. "To me you're a winner no matter what. I promise you a fabulous reward later on when we go back to my place."

Frank held the balls out to Mark. "Want to give it a try?"

Candie clapped her hands and jumped with excitement. "Come on, sweetie. Make your snookins proud of you. Show Wings Falls what a winner you are."

"Snookins?" I asked, turning to my cousin.

She waved a hand at me. "Oh, never mind. You're too tight-laced to understand. It's just a little sweet talk between Mark and me."

My spine stiffened. You'd think I was a Puritan stepping off the Mayflower to hear her talk. "Just because I don't have the flair you do does not make me tight-laced."

Candie raised her shoulders in response. "*Humph.*"

I turned my attention back to Mark. He wound up his arm, took aim, and let the ball fly. The six pumpkins flew off the counter from the force of the ball hitting them.

"Great going, Mark," Frank said and handed a small bear to Candie. She hugged it to her chest. "You're certainly luckier than the last fellow before you two who played this game."

"What happened?" I asked, bending to give a Porkchop and Nina a pat for being so good while we enjoyed ourselves.

"A fellow tried to win his wife one of those bears. She insisted she had to have one. He must have spent at least twenty bucks before giving up. I felt sorry for the guy. I was about to just give him one before his wife pulled him away to see more of the fair."

A thought niggled at my brain. "Do you remember what they looked like?"

Frank stroked his chin. "She was kind of tiny with really red hair. He had quite a paunch. I'd say they were in their midthirties, if I had to venture a guess. "

I turned to Hank. "That sounds like Edgar and his wife. Patsy Ikeda mentioned she'd seen her at the Saratoga Racino. I wonder if she has to win no matter what the game is."

Hank's brow furrowed. "Could that be a reason he charges folks a 'special fee'? To fund her gambling?"

"Maybe," I said.

"Stop, thief!"

Our heads snapped around. I spotted Gladys running across the park as fast as her bird-like legs would carry her, shaking her fist in the air.

CHAPTER TWELVE

———

"Thief, thief. Stop that mangy mutt," Gladys shouted, her orange curls bobbing as she chased after the culprit.

The thief, I presumed, was the brown and white–spotted dog running from her with a fanny pack clutched in its jaws.

Porkchop and Nina joined in the barking frenzy. Unfortunately, I wasn't grasping on to Porkchop's leash tight enough. He pulled it out of my hand and set off on the chase.

Hank shoved Nina's leash at me. "Here, watch her, and I'll see if I can catch that dog."

Candie patted Mark's arm. "Sweetie, help Hank out and catch the sneaky little pup."

Mark leaned over and kissed Candie's cheek. "Anything for my beautiful bride."

Our two fellas took off after the dog, who was evading all attempts to stop him as he darted in and out of the people at the Taste.

Candie frowned. "What would the doggie want with Gladys's fanny pack?"

A light bulb went off in my brain. "Helen complained earlier about the smelly sandwich stuffed in Gladys's fanny pack. Gladys had it nestled alongside the money from the sales of the mug rugs and other items sold at the Loopy Ladies' booth."

Candie bent and petted Nina who, despite all the commotion, stood quietly at my feet sniffing the ground. "Was the sandwich rotten?"

"No, along with the ham was a slice of limburger cheese, and it emitted a pretty pungent odor. Helen wasn't happy about the sandwich residing next to the money."

Candie's auburn curls bounced on her shoulders as she laughed. "This is one time I'd say Helen had a legitimate complaint."

I joined in her laughter. "Yeah, I have to agree with you. Look, Porkchop has caught up with the dog and they're having a tug of war with the strap of Gladys's fanny pack." Candie and I, along with Nina, hurried over to the tree and the two dogs. Mark and Hank were already there, but I thought Porkchop might listen to me better than anyone if he needed to give up the prize he was intent on having.

"Porkchop, what a good boy you are to stop the pup from getting away with Gladys's fanny pack." I dug into my purse for the plastic bag filled with doggie treats I always carried with me.

I took a step forward to offer one to the unknown dog.

Hank put a hand on my arm to stop me. "Here, let me handle this. This dog doesn't know you. I'm not sure how he will react if you try to relieve him of what he thinks is his prize treasure."

I looked up at my brave man and dropped the small bone-shaped treat in his strong hand. My heart skipped a beat at the thought he'd place his safety before mine.

Gladys huffed up next to me. Her sweater hung off her thin shoulders. She rested a gnarled hand over her chest and breathed in shallow gasps of air. "Oh, thank heavens we were able to retrieve our money. What would the dog want with my fanny pack, anyway?"

I smiled. "I'm thinking the dog was after your lunch. I'm sure, and I can tell now it's a he, the dog wasn't after the money you've collected from the sales."

Gladys laughed. "Why, that rascal. I guess he could smell the cheese right through my fanny pack."

I nodded. "It does have a distinct odor."

Candie tugged at the sleeve of my sweater. "Look. Mark and Hank were able to rescue the fanny pack from the dogs. The treats did the trick. I wonder where the dog's owner is. He should have been on a leash."

Mark and Hank walked back to us. Hank held on to Porkchop's leash and grasped his aunt's fanny pack in the other hand while Mark cradled the small dog in his arms.

"Who have you got there, Mark?" I asked as I reached over and scratched the dog's head.

Mark glanced down at the pup nestled in the crook of his arm. "I have no idea, but he's in pitiful shape."

Candie stroked the matted brown and white hair on the dog's head. "The poor fellow looks like he hasn't eaten for a while."

I agreed with my cousin. His skin hung on his body. I could have counted his ribs. He wore no collar or anything to identify who his owner might be. He licked Candie's hand as she continued to croon soothing words to him.

"Mark, he looks like he hasn't eaten in a month of Sundays. Back in Hainted Hollar, if a person treated a dog like this, he'd be taken out to the woodshed for a good thrashing. These sweet things are defenseless, and for a human to treat them in such a manner is criminal."

I nodded in agreement. "Gladys, I believe he snatched your fanny pack because he's starving. Hank, you don't have to arrest him for attempted robbery."

Gladys looked up from inspecting the contents of her fanny pack. "No, I don't think any crime has been committed, other than my sandwich is now a smooshed mess." She tucked the money from the rug sales into a pocket of her sweater then held up the shredded remnants of her ham and limburger cheese sandwich. She pulled the ham out of the sandwich and handed it to the mystery dog. "Here, you might as well have this." The dog gobbled it up faster than a person could blink.

My heart went out to this poor fellow. It was obvious he was hungry. "What are we going to do with him? It doesn't look like his owner is here." I glanced around the park to see if anyone was searching for a lost dog.

Candie pointed to a tall woman walking up to the Sweetie Pie's barbeque line. "We can't leave him to fend for himself. Oh, look, there's Shirley. Since she owns the shelter, she'll know what to do."

We all walked over to the Sweetie Pie's line. "Shirley," I called out.

Shirley turned to us. "What have you got there? Oh, my, this poor pup in pitiful shape." She stroked the dog's head.

Mark nodded. "We believe he's a stray. Has anyone inquired about a missing dog at the shelter recently?"

Shirley's brown ponytail swayed as she shook her head. "No. No one has asked lately, but I'll let you know if they do." The dog nuzzled into the palm of her hand as she continued to pet him.

"In the meantime, can we drop him off at the shelter until someone claims him?" Mark asked.

"What!" Candie screeched. "You're not going to send Cuddles to the shelter. He's coming home with us, where he can get the proper attention. No offense, Shirley. I know you run a reputable shelter for stray animals."

Shirley smiled. "No offense taken. I'll snap a picture of him and post it on our website in case someone *is* looking for him." She reached into her back jeans pocket and pulled out her phone to take the picture.

All of our mouths had dropped open at Candie's pronouncement. "You want to bring this dog home with you? What about Dixie?" I asked, referring to Candie's cat.

"Cuddles. His name is Cuddles," she corrected me.

CHAPTER THIRTEEN

"Yes, I do. Look at him. He needs a loving family that Dixie, Mark, and I can give him. Right, Mark? Right, Cuddles?" Candie placed a finger under the dog's chin. Her violet eyes met Cuddles's liquid chocolate ones.

"Candie, he may already have an owner," Hank said.

Candie cradled the dog close to her. "If he does, the person should be ashamed of themself, letting such a cute thing become so thin and nasty-looking. Shirley, you let us know if someone comes into the shelter looking for him."

Shirley scratched Cuddles between his ears. She loved every pet that came into her shelter as if it were her own. If Cuddles's owner happened to show up to claim him, the person would have a lot of explaining to do before she'd hand him over. "I certainly will, but I have a feeling, from his appearance, he was abandoned."

Candie looked over at Mark and batted her eyelashes. I laughed. My cousin was the only person I knew who could get away with such a feminine act and not look ridiculous. "Mark, can we post on the town's website about a dog being found?"

Mark placed an arm around Candie's shoulder. "Anything you want, sweetheart."

"Hear that, Cuddles? Dadums will make sure you are all ours, legally." Candie squinched up her freckled nose at me.

I did an eyeroll. Did Mark realize his life was going to change with this dog?

"But sweetheart—Cuddles? Can't we name him Spike or Butch? How will it look if when we walk him, I have to call out 'Here, Cuddles'? It won't be good for my image."

Hank and I laughed. I could only imagine Hank shouting Cuddles after a dog. Nope, not going to happen.

"Oh, Mark. You never have to worry about such nonsense. You're more man than anyone I know." Candie glanced over at Hank. "Oh, and you, too, Hank."

I snuggled up against him. "I'll testify to that."

Gladys pointed a finger at the new member of the Hogan family. "Since Mr. Cuddles ate my lunch, what am I going to do? I'm half starved."

Poor Gladys. In all the excitement with Cuddles, I'd completely forgotten about Hank's aunt. She stood behind us clutching her sweater to her thin chest. The wind blew her baggy pull-on pants against her thin legs and tousled her orange curls about her head.

Porkchop walked over and laid his small head on her rubber boot–clad feet. My heart melted at the compassion he showed her. "I'm sorry, Gladys. Let's go over to Franny's booth and get you some barbeque. How does a juicy pulled pork sandwich sound?"

Now that the excitement of chasing down a runaway dog was over, the fair had resumed its activity. The line at Franny's booth was forming again, as were the lines and crowds at all the other vendors.

"It sounds wonderful. Pookie Bear and I try to go to Sweetie Pie's at least once a week. Oh, but the money in my fanny pack belonged to the Loopy Ladies. I left my wallet at the booth."

"Don't worry, Aunt Gladys. It will be my treat," Hank said.

I smiled up at Hank. He was such a gentleman.

Gladys patted his arm. "You are a dear."

We all walked over to Franny's booth and got in line. Luckily, the line wasn't too long yet. Five people waited in front of us, all anticipating some mouthwatering pulled pork on a bun.

Aaron stood next to a portable grill stirring the barbeque while Joy handed him a paper plate with an open bun for him to fill. Franny was at the end of the table acting as hostess, chatting with people and accepting payment for the sandwiches.

I laughed. "You have quite an assembly line going."

Aaron wore an apron emblazoned with the words *Sweetie Pie's Cafe*. "With the crowd we've got today, you've got to have a system, and I think we work pretty well together."

Joy smiled. "It's all Aaron's doing. He organized us so we're a smooth-running team."

"Good for you, Aaron."

I heard the pride in Hank's voice. In spite of all his grumbling about his brother and the antics he pulled at times, I knew he was really proud of him.

"Aunt Gladys needs a sandwich. Cuddles managed to eat the one she brought from home." Hank nodded towards Candie and Mark.

Joy frowned. "Cuddles?"

"Yes, it's what I've named this sweet pup." Candie turned the dog so Aaron and Joy could see his face.

Aaron coughed. I was sure to hide the laughter bubbling up his throat. "Um, hi Cuddles. Nice to meet you. Candie, do you and Mark want a sandwich, too?"

Candie stroked the fur on Cuddles's back. "We'll stop back. I want to get over to the Fur Babies' booth and buy this pup a collar and leash. Right, Cuddlie Wuddlie? How about a nice rhinestone collar? I know you'll love rhinestones as much as your momma."

I rolled my eyes. A truer statement Candie had never made—rhinestones were her middle name. I think she sported bling on everything but her underwear, and I wouldn't put it past her to have some bling there, too. Not that I really wanted to know.

"But Candie, I'm starving. Couldn't we get some barbeque first and then buy the collar and leash?" From Mark's hangdog look, he did look famished.

Candie placed a hand on Mark's cheek. "Yes, sweetums. Right after we outfit Cuddles, we'll come back and get you one of Franny's fabulous barbeque sandwiches. Joy, you'll have some left in about a half an hour, won't you?"

Joy smiled. "I'm sure we will. In fact, I'll place some aside for the two of you."

"Oh, thank you. You are a darling. Come on, Mark. Fur Babies is a popular booth."

Mark turned to us and shrugged his shoulders. His stomach rumbled as if to emphasis his hunger. "I guess I'll see you two around the park."

Candie slipped her arm through his then leaned over and kissed his cheek.

I laughed as they walked towards Fur Babies' booth. "Mark is a goner. I think he'd walk through fire for her."

Hank leaned down and kissed my cheek. "I can think of someone else who would walk through fire for the one they love."

My cheeks grew warm. "I love you, too," I whispered back.

Porkchop and Nina jumped at our feet, drawing us back to our mission at hand—a barbeque sandwich for Aunt Gladys.

Gladys poked my shoulder. "You two are sweet lovebirds, but I'm starved."

I blinked and focused on our task at hand. "Hank, Gladys is about to perish if you don't get her a sandwich."

Hank laughed. "Aaron, you'd better hand a sandwich over to your aunt."

"Sure enough, big bro."

Gladys shook a gnarled finger at Aaron. "And no skimping on the barbeque, either."

Joy's ponytail shook as she laughed. "We'd never think of it, Mrs. O'Malley. Would you and Sam like one, too?" she asked Hank.

Hank turned to me and raised his eyebrows.

"I'll pass until later. I'm still full of the sandwich we got at The Round Up's booth."

Hank nodded. "I have to agree. You'll save some for us, too?"

Aaron handed Gladys her plate. "We sure will. Enjoy Franny's secret recipe, Aunt Gladys, and be sure to vote for us for the best barbeque at the Taste of Wings Falls."

CHAPTER FOURTEEN

───────

I scanned the area set aside for eating for an empty picnic table so Gladys could sit and eat her sandwich. The only table with any room to enjoy her lunch was under a maple tree about ten feet away. The problem was, Carol and Edgar Jensen were also sitting at the table, and after what had taken place earlier with Aaron and Joy, I didn't feel like making small talk with them as Gladys ate her meal.

I touched her thin arm and pointed to the picnic area. "Gladys, it looks like the picnic tables are all full. How about Porkchop and I walk you back to the Loopy Ladies' booth, where you can sit and enjoy your lunch?"

"That sounds like a wonderful idea. When I get back to the booth, I'll give Pookie Bear a call and see if he'd like some barbeque, too."

"He was manning a *hit the pumpkins* table a bit ago. Where is he now?"

Gladys laughed. "He's volunteering all over the park today. He's at Mark's table now, handing out flyers and answering any questions folks might have about our great mayor." Her hand holding her plate trembled.

I held out my hand. "Here. Let me take that for you. There are a lot of tree roots you could stumble over, and with the crowd here, someone could knock into you on the way back to our booth." I turned to Hank. "You don't mind making yourself busy for a little while, do you?"

"Of course not. There's plenty of sights to take in. I noticed Al's Sports Shop has a booth. I'd like to check out his fishing equipment. Maybe stock up on a few things for this coming spring when the trout are running again. Do you want me to take Porkchop with me?"

Al Gorman owned Al's Sports Shop, a popular spot in town for all the anglers in Wings Falls. Hank had taken up fly fishing after moving here from Albany last year, and as his fellow fishermen would say, he was "hooked."

I reached up and kissed Hank on the cheek. "You have fun talking fishing to Al. I'll meet you at the Loopy Ladies' booth later. Come on, Porkchop. Let's get Gladys settled before she perishes from hunger."

Gladys swatted at my arm. "Oh, you're silly but such a dear to an old lady like me."

"Gladys, when I reach your age—which I know is a well-guarded secret—if I have half your energy, I'll be happy."

Gladys laughed as the three of us—Gladys, Porkchop, and I—strolled across the park, being careful to dodge costumed children running amongst the booths and fairgoers munching on cider doughnuts and engrossed in conversations with each other.

As we approached the Loopy Ladies' booth, I was happy to see a good-sized group of people admiring our handiwork.

Helen Garber stood behind the table with Cookie Harrington, one of the younger members of our group. She worked as the receptionist at the Wings Falls Animal Hospital but arranged her schedule so she could join us for our Monday morning hooking sessions at The Ewe.

I pointed to the empty spaces on our tent's walls, where rugs had hung earlier this morning. "Hi, Cookie. I see you and Helen have been busy."

A smile split Cookie's face. Her black curls bounced about her dark face as she nodded. "Yes, we have. If this keeps up, breakdown this evening will be very easy. There won't be anything to take home."

"That would be wonderful if we sold out," I said, trying to hold on to Porkchop's leash and Gladys's plate. His nose was twitching in the direction of the barbeque. I knew he was hoping some of it would fall his way. "Gladys. How about you take a seat and enjoy your lunch?" I pointed to a metal chair sitting at the back of the tent.

Helen finished making change for a customer who'd bought a small pumpkin rug I had hooked.

"Here you are, Gladys." I waited until she was settled in the folding chair before I handed her the plate.

She rested it on her lap then took a bite of her sandwich. "Hmmm… This has a unique taste to it. Franny must have changed up her recipe. But it still hits the spot. I'll have to sample The Smiling Pig's and The Round Up's barbeque before I can make a final decision." She swiped her tongue around her lips to capture any stray barbeque sauce.

"It certainly is going to be a hard decision picking the winning barbeque. They all have a taste special to themselves." I kept Porkchop on a short leash so Gladys could enjoy her sandwich in peace without Porkchop giving her his sad eyes and begging for a taste.

"Sam, could you give me a hand here? I need to go to the ladies' room," Helen called over her shoulder.

Porkchop and I walked over and stood between Helen and Cookie. "Oh, sorry. I should have been helping you with the crowd gathering around the booth. There's no need to hurry back. I can stay for a while. Why don't you take a break and enjoy the fair?"

"Well, if you think you can handle it." Helen reached under the table for her purse. A large leather bag in bright orange. Nothing about Helen was subtle—from her flaming red hair to her lemon-yellow shirt and lime-green sweater.

I gritted my teeth to stop the words that really wanted to spill out. "Oh, I think we can manage, right Cookie?"

I could tell she was biting the inside of her cheek to keep from laughing out loud as Helen walked away. "She really is one of a kind."

"Yes, she is, but then again, so are a lot of the Loopy Ladies. In case you haven't noticed in your short time as a member of our group."

"*Humph!*" came from behind us. "The dear Lord broke the mold for stubborn and opinionated when he created that woman."

Now I did laugh out loud. "If you say so."

With a sharp nod of her head, Gladys said, "I say so. That woman would give a man-eating alligator indigestion."

"Hi ladies. What do you think?"

"Oh, hi yourself, Candie." She stood in front of the table. Cuddles, the dear puppy, squirmed as she clutched him to her chest. He now sported a rhinestone collar and a violet leash studded with rhinestones.

"I see you found a little something for Cuddles. Where's Mark?" I reached over the table and patted Cuddles.

"He's back at his table handing out flyers and encouraging people to sign up for the town's website so they'll be up-to-date on the goings on in Wings Falls.

"Can I take your picture?"

I looked past Candie's shoulder to see Rob Anderson, the reporter from the *Tribune* who had taken the pictures of the winners of the pet costume parade. He had his camera clutched in his hands.

Candie swiveled towards him. "You want to take my Cuddles's picture? Oh, goodie. Now both my babies will have their pictures in the paper. Cuddles, you and your sister will be famous."

"I don't know about famous, but his picture will be in tonight's paper in the section featuring the Taste of Wings Falls. My editor thought it would be a great human-interest story.

Candie leaned her cheek against Cuddles. "Now smile, Cuddles, for the nice cameraman."

A groan came from the back of the tent. I turned to see Gladys clutching her throat and turning a green to match Helen's sweater. "Gladys, what's the matter? You don't look well."

Sweat dotted Gladys's forehead. "I don't feel very well, and I'm dizzy. I think I might faint."

CHAPTER FIFTEEN

———

I dropped Porkchop's leash and ran over to a pale and swaying Gladys. "Gladys!" I shouted as I placed an arm around her to steady her on her chair. An unusual smell caught my nose as I grabbed the plate of barbeque from her limp fingers before it slid to the ground. It was an odd scent but one I knew I had smelled and recently. I lifted the plate to my nose and took another sniff. Of course. I had just purchased a bottle of it from Montana Casey— lavender. Now why would Franny's barbeque be laced with lavender?

Cookie hurried over to my side. "What is the matter? What can I do to help Mrs. O'Malley?" Even though Cookie was the receptionist at the animal hospital, she dealt with enough emergencies that she was coolheaded in a situation like Gladys's.

"Candie, call 9-1-1, and then call Hank and tell him to come to our booth ASAP." Candie placed Cuddles on the ground and dug into her purse for her bejeweled phone.

I glared at Rob Anderson as he snapped pictures of Gladys. Was he so desperate for a story he would take advantage of an elderly woman in distress? "Rob, can you give Mrs. O'Malley some privacy? There isn't anything to see here."

Candie walked into the tent and stood in front of Gladys to block Rob's view of poor Gladys as she swayed in her chair. "Well, bless his heart. I'm sure his momma taught him better than to take advantage of an older woman in her time of distress." Cuddles and Porkchop growled at the reporter, giving their opinion of the reporter's actions.

Red flushed up Rob's face at Candie's rebuke. "Um, sure, ma'am. Is there anything I can do to help?"

Gladys placed a shaking hand on her forehead. "Can you go over to the mayor's table and tell Frank Gilbert I need him?"

"Will do," Rob said and turned on his heels and fled towards Mark's table, saying, "Excuse me, excuse me," as he bumped into people in his hurried retreat.

Porkchop's nose twitched the air at the plate of barbeque I held out of his reach. If, as I suspected, there was something in the barbeque that had made Gladys ill, I certainly didn't want him to eat any of it.

I turned my attention back to Gladys. "Candie is calling for help. Just hang in there. Do you feel like you're going to be sick?" My heart ached to see my usually strong and independent neighbor looking so frail and vulnerable right now. She barely had the strength to hold up her head. It lolled against her thin chest.

In a voice slightly above a whisper, she replied, "I feel so weak, and my stomach is churning a mile a minute. I don't want to make a mess of things, but I think I might throw up."

"Cookie, take Gladys's plate and hand me a paper bag from the stack we used to place our sold items in."

Cookie was quick to respond. She placed the plate on the table and flipped open a bag for me, which I promptly gave to Gladys, who filled it with the contents of her stomach.

Sensing Gladys's distress, Porkchop sat at her feet and whined.

"I'm sorry to be a bother to you young ladies. I don't know what's come over me."

I was afraid I might know—Franny's barbeque was tainted with an ingredient I suspected might be lavender. It couldn't be the "added touch" that Joy mentioned Aaron had added to the recipe…could it? I glanced towards the uneaten portion of the sandwich sitting on the table then up at Cookie and Candie. "We'll have to make sure to preserve what Gladys hasn't eaten."

Cookie raised an eyebrow at me. "Sure, but how come?"

I hated to admit it, but it was a distinct possibility. "I think someone may have sabotaged Franny's barbeque." It had to be someone other than Aaron. I wouldn't believe he'd place something harmful in the barbeque.

Cookie's eyes widened. "Would winning first place at the Taste of Wings Falls be so important to someone they would endanger people's health?"

I shrugged. "I think that's a question for the police."

"Does someone need help here?"

I looked up to see Jim Turner accompanied by Jane Burrows. Jim was the fire chief but also a licensed EMT.

"I heard a call go out over our scanner you have an emergency here," he said.

"Yes, Gladys O'Malley has become ill, and I think she should be checked out."

Jim rounded the table and walked over to Gladys's side. I got up so he could assess her condition. "What's ailing you today, Mrs. O'Malley?"

"Now don't you all go making such a fuss over me. I think it may have been something I ate."

"Sweet Cheeks, Sweet Cheeks. What's the matter? That reporter fellow said to get over here ASAP. He said you were at death's door." A frazzled-looking Frank Gilbert burst into the tent. He rushed past Jim and knelt on the ground next to Gladys. He grabbed her hand and cradled it in his.

"Sweet Cheeks?" Candie whispered out of the side of her mouth.

A smile tugged at my lips. "What can I say? He's Pookie Bear to her."

I hated to break up this love fest, but I thought Jim should check on Gladys's condition. "Gladys, let Jim have a look at you."

She stared up at me. "You're all making a fuss out of nothing."

"Humor me. Let Jim check out the 'nothing'."

"Aunt Gladys, listen to Sam. You know my momma would have a fit if you didn't do as you were told."

I turned in surprise to see Hank standing behind me with Nina at his feet. Cuddles and Porkchop wagged their tails in greeting to Nina. Hank's mother was Gladys's baby sister. But from the stories he had told me, Gladys usually deferred to her advice or, as she referred to them, her commands.

"Oh. That sister of mine. All right, Jim, have your way with me."

Jim asked Gladys the usual questions to see how she felt. Was she light-headed? Did she have any pain? He took her pulse and listened to her heart with the stethoscope he pulled from his back pocket.

Tears started to flow down my cheeks as I watched Frank standing in a corner wringing his hands. Worry etched his craggy face. He and Gladys may be what most people referred to as elderly, but their love was as fresh and young as a teenager's.

Hank placed an arm around my shoulder and pulled me up against his strong body. I looked at him and tried to draw some strength from him. He placed a kiss on the top of my head.

"She'll be all right, won't she?" I whispered.

Hank smiled. "She's too tough an old bird not to be."

I poked him in the ribs. "Don't let her hear you calling her an old bird."

He nodded. "Yeah, she'd tell my ma, and then I'd hear it from her, too."

I glanced over at the plate of barbeque sitting on the table. In all the excitement, I had forgotten to tell Hank my suspicions about it possibly being tampered with. "Hank, the barbeque from Sweetie Pie's…"

He frowned. "Yeah, what about it?"

"I think it's the reason Gladys got ill. It has an odd smell about it."

"Odd in what way? Maybe they changed up their recipe."

"No, I think there's more to it than that. It has the smell of lavender to it."

Hank walked over to the plate and held it up to his nose. He took a sniff then looked at me. "Lavender."

"Sweet Cheeks!" Frank screeched.

My attention shifted back to Frank. My hand flew to my mouth.

"Here, take Nina's leash." Hank shoved his dog's leash into my hand then rushed over to Gladys as she lay unconscious on the ground.

CHAPTER SIXTEEN

————

"My Sweet Cheeks." Tears ran down Frank's lined face as he knelt next to Gladys, stroking her hand. Her face was whiter than one of Memaw Parker's sheets.

My heart thudded in my chest. Had Franny's pulled pork made Gladys sick? Why did her barbeque have a hint of lavender? Was this the something new Aaron had added to the recipe? If so, wouldn't he check to make sure there would be no adverse side effects to it? Although lavender was often used in cooking, I learned from Montana Tracey that a person must use edible-grade lavender and not the lavender used in the essentials oils I loved so much. How desperate was Sweetie Pie's to win the cook-off? The prize money of five-hundred dollars and a trophy shaped like a flapping chicken certainly wasn't worth making people sick. Questions tumbled around my brain as I watched Frank and Hank kneel next to Gladys's prone body.

Hank had removed his sweater, rolled it in a ball, and placed it under Gladys's head. He glanced up at me. Worry etched his handsome face.

She stirred and opened her eyes. "What the blazes is happening? Why am I on the ground? Pookie Bear, help me up." She tried to push herself up on her elbows. This, I hoped, was a good sign, that she was no longer unconscious and back to her feisty self.

Frank placed a hand on her shoulder and tried to restrain her from getting up. "Now, Sweet Cheeks, you need to rest a few minutes, You became sick and passed out."

Gladys looked around her. "That's silly. I'll be fine. Anyone got some Pepto?"

Jim Turner stood and talked into the mic attached to his shoulder. "Dispatch, send an ambulance to the Loopy Ladies' booth ASAP. We have an elderly lady who became unconscious from an unknown cause. What? Roger. Got that. Ten-four." Jim knelt next to

Hank and spoke in a hushed tone to him. Hank's eyebrows rose as he turned his head and scanned the park. He nodded and rose from the ground.

Cookie, Candie, and I lurked at the opening of the tent looking helpless. We tended to the dogs, making sure they didn't get in the way. Not that I was very good in an emergency situation. Panic was my middle name when something dire happened. I might co-own a funeral parlor with my ex, but my role was now strictly a money investment. Unlike when we were first married and I manned the office. Now I rarely made an appearance at the Do Drop.

Hank walked over to me. "We have an emergency on our hands."

I couldn't agree more. "I know, but Gladys seems to be recovering." I pointed to his aunt.

Hank shook his head. "No, it appears more people are getting sick after eating Franny's barbeque. I have to get over to her booth and shut it down."

I turned to the picnic area, and sure enough, men and women were slumped on the picnic benches, clutching their stomachs and groaning out loud. Luckily, I didn't see any children amongst them. Ambulances pulled up to the Taste, and before they parked, EMTs carrying medical bags jumped out of the vehicles and ran towards the affected people. One young fellow hurried over to Gladys.

He rounded the table and came to a halt before her. "Ma'am, I understand you have been ill. Do you mind if I see what's wrong?"

Gladys laughed and patted her orange curls. "Sonny, only a bit of indigestion and a slight upset stomach. Your chief here has already taken care of the matter." Gladys pointed to Jim. "If you all will lend me a hand so I can get to my feet and onto the chair over there, I'll be fine."

Frank, along with the EMT, helped Gladys to stand and guided her to the folding chair. "Darlin', let the young man do his job. After all, we're not so spry anymore."

Gladys swatted at Frank's arm. "What are you saying, we're not so spry anymore? Speak for yourself, you old coot."

Those of us gathered in the tent laughed. Gladys may have felt ill a few moments ago, but she still had her sense of humor.

"Sugar, what can we do about all of this?" Candie swept a ringed finger towards the scene unfolding before us at the picnic tables with the EMTs attending to the ill.

"I think the Wings Falls Emergency crew has everything under control, but I want to go over to Franny's booth. I know she's going to be devastated by what is going on." I turned to Cookie. "Can you watch the booth while Candie and I check on Franny?"

"No problem. I'll stay and make sure Mrs. O'Malley is taken care of."

Gladys waved a hand at us to dismiss my concern. "Don't go fussing over me. I'll be fine. Maybe someone can fetch me a ginger ale. I know it will settle my stomach in no time flat."

*   *   *

"Franny, how are you doing?" Candie stood next to me as I watched officers from the Wings Falls Police Department cart away Franny's pans of barbeque. Aaron leaned against one of the tent's support poles with his arm around a weeping Joy.

Franny positioned herself at the end of a table with her hands on her slim hips. Anger seethed from her body. I could almost reach out and touch it. "Why are they picking on my pulled pork and not the barbeque from The Smiling Pig or The Round Up? What makes them so sure it was my food making people sick?"

My heart went out to her. She had a fabulous reputation for serving up home-cooked, Southern-style food. A line usually snaked out the front door of Sweetie Pie's, especially on the weekends. It certainly was Candie's and my favorite place to enjoy breakfast Sunday mornings after church. "Franny, did you make any last-minute changes to your recipe? Maybe add new ingredients to spice it up?"

Franny frowned. "What are you talking about? It's the same recipe I brought north with me over fifteen years ago. My momma perfected it way before then for the church socials we used to attend. She even entered it in the county fair held every August in our area. She won a blue ribbon for it. Why would I change a winning recipe?"

Why indeed, I thought. "You sure nothing new was added?" I asked as officers carted off square aluminum pans containing the barbeque in question.

"Why would I do that? The recipe is a winner in my opinion. I knew it would bring home this year's trophy for me. I even had a special shelf made to display it on in the restaurant."

Porkchop tugged at his leash. He was becoming restless with all the standing around he was doing, first at the Loopy Ladies' booth and now at Franny's. "Be patient a little longer, Porkie, and then we'll go for a walk."

Franny ran a hand through her hair, dislodging it from the scrunchie holding it out of her face. She turned to Aaron and Joy. "Did either of you try to fancy up my recipe?"

Aaron stood up straighter. "No way, Franny. Like you're telling Sam, why would we mess with a winning recipe?"

I turned to Aaron. "Joy mentioned that you tweaked the recipe a bit."

He glanced at Joy. A guilty look crossed his face. "I didn't do a thing to her recipe. Why mess with perfection? I know I told you I added a few special spices to give it a new twist, but I couldn't bring myself to do it. I'm sorry, Joy. I just wanted to impress you."

Joy walked over to her aunt and placed an arm over her shoulder. "Aunt Franny, neither Aaron nor I would do a thing to your famous barbeque. It is perfect."

Candie shifted next to me. I could tell she was as uncomfortable as I was questioning Franny. We both considered Franny a friend and found it awkward asking about her recipe. But as things stood now, it looked like the police would have a lot more questions for her than we did.

"What do you know about my barbeque you aren't telling me?" Franny asked. Tears streaked down her dark cheeks.

I twisted Porkchop's leash in my hand. "Weeellll. When Gladys became sick, I took a sniff of the sandwich she had gotten from you, and I detected a lavender scent to it."

Franny's eyes widened. "Lavender? That can't be possible. In all the years I've been preparing my barbeque, I never used lavender as an ingredient. Not once."

"Could someone have slipped some in your sauce when you weren't looking?" Candie asked.

Now that was a possibility I hadn't thought of.

CHAPTER SEVENTEEN

Aaron shoved his hands into the front pockets of his jeans. "Well, when your dog"—he pointed to Cuddles—"and Porkchop raced through the crowd earlier, things did get a little hectic."

"What do you mean?" I asked, looking down at Porkchop.

"They ran right through our line of people. Joy and I got distracted watching the fuss the dogs were causing," Aaron said.

"Were you distracted enough someone could have slipped something in the pulled pork you were serving?"

Joy nodded. "Sam, they could have. We were all too busy watching what was going on with the dogs chasing each other, and at that point our customers were pretty scattered."

"What would anyone have to gain from tainting your food?" Candie asked. Cuddles, true to his name, lay snuggled in her arms, snoring softly.

Franny stood straighter and puffed up with pride. "If they beat us. And I'm sure we had the winning recipe—bragging rights, a trophy to display in their restaurant and, most of all, increased customers wanting to taste this year's winner of the Taste of Wings Falls Best Barbeque."

"Increased customers?" Candie said.

My eyes widened. "It could help solve the money problems both The Round Up and The Smiling Pig are having."

At that moment, Nina yipped as if to add her agreement to my statement. I bent and scratched her wrinkled head. "You're right, girl."

Franny stuck out her chin. "Since whoever did this knocked me out of the competition, it eliminates me as a suspect."

I wanted to think it did, but what if Franny sabotaged her own food to throw the suspicion on the other two restaurants and get the sympathy of the good citizens of Wings Falls so they would patronize Sweetie Pie's? Nah. I shook my head. She wouldn't do that, but I couldn't see the owners of The Round Up and The Smiling Pig messing with their own food, either. So, who?

"I hate to break up your conversation, but I need to question Franny, Joy, and Aaron about what has happened here today."

I jerked. My hand flew to my heart. I'd been so engrossed with our conversation with Franny, I hadn't heard Hank come up behind me. "Geez. You scared me to death."

Porchop and Nina jumped at Hank's legs. He bent and scratched both of them between their ears.

Hank and Mark stood side by side. "I'm sorry. I didn't mean to frighten you."

I placed a hand on his arm. "That's okay. How are things? Have you discovered what is making the people sick?"

Hank shook his head. "We questioned both Clint and Bill Collins. They haven't had anyone whose eaten their sandwiches become ill. We've taken a sample of what they've served to be analyzed at a lab in Albany, same as my guys have done with Franny's. Unfortunately, since we don't know what made people ill, we've had to close down the competition."

I thought it was a good move for the police department. I glanced around the park and noticed that anyone who had appeared to be ill was now being attended by an EMT. Most of the victims were already up and walking around, having rid their stomachs of the barbeque. None appeared to have fainted like Gladys. The fair was once again busy with shoppers who hadn't been affected by the pulled pork sandwiches, but everyone appeared to be whispering about what had happened. Being a small town, this would be on the Wings Falls gossip mill for at least the next week.

Mark stepped forward. "This is work for your department, Hank. I'm more of a third wheel here right now. Why don't I take the ladies and pups home? Let me know what you find out."

"Will do," Hank said then looked at me. "Would you mind watching Nina again tonight? I have a feeling this is going to take a while."

I reached up and kissed Hank's cheek. "Porchop and I will take good care of your baby. Don't be too hard on Aaron. I know he, Franny, and Joy had nothing to do with this."

Hank hugged me to his side. "I certainly hope you're right."

As we walked away, Candie reached for my hand and gave it a squeeze. "This has to be hard on him, having to question his brother, but I know Aaron is innocent."

"That's what I told him before we left, but he has to do his duty," I said as we walked down the leaf-strewn sidewalk to Mark's car.

As I settled Porkchop, Nina, and myself into the rear seat of Mark's red Ford Escape, weariness lay on my shoulders like a lead shawl. Candie sat next to Mark, cooing to her Cuddles. I leaned back against the headrest and stroked Porkchop's and Nina's backs as they vied for a spot on my lap. My eyes drifted shut as I wondered how a day starting out so sunny and full of fun could have turned so horribly wrong.

* * *

"We're here, darling. Do you want me to help you into the house with your puppies?"

"What? What?" I blinked and rubbed my eyes. True, it was only a short drive from the Wings Falls park to my house, but it seemed as if I'd just settled into the car, and we were now sitting in the driveway of my ranch-style home.

"I'll be fine, Candie. I guess the excitement of the day has worn me out. I think I'll give the dogs a bite to eat and then we'll all take a nap."

Candie twisted in her seat so she was facing me. "If you're sure. You can come home with Mark and me and wait there for a call from Hank."

I shook my head. What I really wanted was for Hank to join me and the pups snuggled on my sofa, gazing into a roaring fire. Maybe, fingers crossed, this still could happen. "No, you and Mark head on home. We'll be fine. Hopefully, Hank will stop over later on." I climbed out of Mark's car and reached back in to help Porkchop and Nina. Once all paws were on the ground, I leaned in Candie's window and gave her a kiss on the cheek. "Thank you for the ride home. Now scoot and try to enjoy what is left of the day." I waved as Mark backed out of my driveway.

I tugged on the dogs' leashes. "Come on. Let's get a bite to eat then settle in for a call from Hank." Porkchop's and Nina's tails wagged like metronomes gone crazy. I swore these two understood any word having to do with food—like eat, treat, kibble.

* * *

"What the…? Are you guys hungry already? I just fed you…" I glanced at the schoolhouse clock hanging next to my fireplace. I rubbed my eyes. "It can't be that late." I looked out my front window, and sure enough, darkness was starting to descend over Wings Falls and the hands on my clock indicated it was nearly seven o'clock. Porkchop and Nina sat next to my sofa and whined. They give me their best puppy eyes.

I reached down and scratched between Nina's ears. "Your daddy hasn't called. Maybe if we take a walk over to the park, we'll catch a glimpse of him. I'm not counting on it, but it is worth a try. Remember, if he's there, no getting into trouble. He has enough to worry about. How about some kibble first? " The dogs trotted next to me as I led them into the kitchen.

CHAPTER EIGHTEEN

———

"Now that your tummies are full, how about that walk to the park to see if Hank is still there?" Both Nina and Porkchop cocked their heads at me. I patted my thigh, and with tails wagging, they followed me to the front door. I opened the closet next to my front door and reached in for my down vest. Once the sun set, the temperature would drop. I would need the extra warmth it provided. Porkchop's tail thumped the tile floor of my entryway in anticipation of a romp outside.

I bent and clipped on his leash. "You're going to have to behave like a gentleman. It'll be a handful walking the two of you together. No tugging and pulling when you see a squirrel or if any other critter crosses your path." Nina sat patiently waiting her turn to be hooked up. Once everyone was leashed and ready for a stroll in the park, I grabbed my head lamp off the table sitting across from the front door. I turned it on and slipped it onto my head. A fashion statement it wasn't, but it enabled me to have my hands free while holding on to the dogs.

Stepping outside, I glanced over at Gladys's house and hoped she was feeling better after eating her pulled pork sandwich earlier today. I knew she was in good hands with her Pookie Bear tending to her. I marveled at the bright orange moon rising over Wings Falls. The meteorologists called it a harvest moon. I called it beautiful. My head lamp emitted enough light for me to navigate the sidewalks leading to the park. I was glad I'd chosen to wear my down vest, as the temperature had dipped quite a bit since this afternoon.

I set a brisk pace for the dogs to get our body temperatures up. As we approached the park, Porkchop sniffed the air and started to whine. "What's the matter, boy?" Something had the hairs on his back standing on end. I bent and ran my hand down his back to smooth it down, but his fur refused to lie flat. Nina became agitated, too. She chimed in Porkchop's whining chorus.

People arguing from the far side of the park made me snap my head in the direction of the voices. Who else beside me was out walking tonight? Maybe Hank was still here in the park, but would he be arguing with someone? I doubted it. Before I'd left the house, I'd tried his number, but it had gone to his voicemail. My head lamp shone on a figure running towards me. A shiver ran through me, and this time it wasn't from the cold. Suddenly, I felt defenseless. Here I was, standing with two small dogs, by myself, on a deserted sidewalk in Wings Falls. My town did have the nickname of Hometown USA, but bad things could happen in even the safest of towns. I swallowed hard. After all, we'd had three murders since last year. "Now stop it, Sam," I chided myself.

As the runner approached, I let out the breath I had been holding. My shaking hands calmed down, and Porkchop and Nina stopped whining and wagged their tails in greeting. "Hi, Aaron. Out for an evening run?"

Aaron bent and ruffled the fur on both dogs' heads. "Yeah, I needed to blow off some steam. It's not fun getting grilled by your big brother for supposedly causing people to become ill."

"I guess it isn't, but he is only doing his job." My heart ached for how Hank must have felt questioning his baby brother.

Aaron shoved his hands in the pockets of his worn hoodie. "Yeah, I know. So, instead of going to the nearest bar and getting drunk, I thought I'd work it out by taking a jog around town."

I nodded. Maybe Aaron was growing up after all. "Good choice. How's Joy doing?"

"She's at home with Franny. As you can gather, Franny is pretty upset the police think her food made fairgoers sick."

I could only imagine how devastated Franny was. She'd spent years building up her reputation in Wings Falls. Something like this could destroy her and her business. "I would certainly think she is very upset. Sweetie Pie's is her life."

A shout interrupted our conversation. Our heads whipped in its direction. "Who is that? I heard arguing from that direction earlier," I said. This time, Porkchop and Nina did more than whine. They started to bark.

"I don't know. I ran past there a few minutes ago, and everything seemed all right. There were two people talking, but other than them, the park was deserted except for me taking my run.

"Did you recognize them?"

Aaron shook his head. "Nope. I was just concentrating on my run and trying to get my cool back after what happened with Hank questioning me and that jerk Jensen making a pass at Joy. That guy really had me steamed. If Joy hadn't been there, I might have done something more than shove him." He looked back toward where the voices had been arguing. "Maybe I should go see what's happening."

"How about we call the police first. Things have been too crazy today." As I reached into my pocket for my phone, I heard a car screeching down the road.

Aaron turned and jogged back in the direction of the shout. "Let me check things out first," he called over his shoulder.

I shook my head. I thought it was a foolish thing for Aaron to do, but that was youth for you.

Porkchop pulled at his leash. He wanted to follow Aaron. "Wait, Porkchop. We don't know what has happened."

When Porkchop refused to stay put, I trotted along after him in the direction of where Scooter Dickenson had parked his truck containing his prize-winning pumpkin on the grounds of Wings Falls Park. As we approached, Porkchop's whines turned into full-throated barks. Aaron stood next to the truck, pointing at the sidewalk. I trained my head lamp to where he pointed —Scooter's pumpkin. But it no longer rested on the back of his truck. Now it lay on the ground with a pair of feet sticking out from under it.

I felt light-headed and started to sway. Aaron noticed my wobbly stance and reached over and placed an arm around my shoulder to steady me. "Who do you think it is?"

I ran a trembling hand through my curls. "I have no idea. Is he alive?" The feet jutting out from under the pumpkin were definitely men's, or at least, they wore a man's style shoe. I reached into my pocket for my phone and punched in 9-1-1. When I was connected to the operator, I informed her there was a serious accident in the park involving a victim and a pumpkin. At first, I thought she believed I was a prank caller. I had to admit my call did sound a little far-fetched. I mean, how many calls must they receive featuring a deadly pumpkin? They'd be talking about this one at the dispatch center for a while.

Aaron walked around the pumpkin. He bent and leaned his shoulder into it and gave the pumpkin a couple of shoves, but to no avail. The pumpkin didn't budge an inch, which didn't surprise me. Scooter had boasted it weighed over 2,000 pounds.

Porkchop and Nina stopped barking but were busy sniffing the victim's feet. I tugged on their leashes to pull them back a few inches. Porkchop wasn't very happy and stared up at me as if to say, *When we walked past this giant pumpkin earlier during the fair, I tried to tell you this gourd was going to be trouble.* Maybe he sensed something tragic would happen when he barked at the pumpkin this morning.

I held my phone up to Aaron. "Let me try Hank again. I called him earlier, but it went to his voicemail."

A scowl crossed Aaron's face, one so like Hank's with the lock of brown hair that refused to stay in place. "He was probably busy cross-examining me about the barbeque."

I placed a hand on his arm. "Aaron, like I said before, he's only doing his job. Now let me see if I can get ahold of him." As I held my phone to my ear and listened to it ringing, I heard the sound of sirens approaching us.

I was about to disconnect when he picked up. "Hi, Sam, sorry I missed all your earlier calls. It's been a long day."

I cradled the phone next to my ear. "I'm sure it has, but I have some bad news."

Hank's voice immediately changed to one of urgency. "What's happened? Are you all right? Are those sirens I hear?"

My voice shook, but I refused to dissolve into a puddle of tears. "Yes, I'm fine, but I'm here in the park with Aaron and the dogs. We have stumbled on a dead body."

"Again?" Hank asked. Disbelief laced his voice.

"Yes. Again," I replied. I didn't believe it myself.

CHAPTER NINETEEN

———

"What did big bro have to say? I bet he wasn't very happy."
Aaron bent over and tried to give the huge pumpkin another shove.

I was getting agitated with Aaron's attitude. "Cut him a
break, Aaron. Of course he's not happy we've found a dead person,
but he was also very concerned. He cares about us. Don't go messing
with the pumpkin. Let the police handle it. I see a cop car turning the
corner right now." A black and white pulled up to the curb. The door
was flung open, and I groaned.

Once again, Porkchop's hair stood up on his back and a
growl rumbled up his throat.

Two uniformed policemen exited the car. From behind the
wheel emerged a tall muscled black man whose name tag read Reed.
I'd become acquainted with him when he was involved in another
murder investigation this past summer.

The cause of my groan swung his legs out of the passenger
side of the patrol car. Sergeant Joe Peters—my childhood nemesis.
Joe and I went through school together, but that's as far as our
friendship extended. He walked over to the pumpkin and bent down.
"Geez, this guy won't be celebrating any more Halloweens. He looks
like a bowl of Jell-O."

My stomach lurched. That was smooth Joe for you.

He glanced over at me. "I see you're smack dab in the middle
of another death. You have the bad habit of turning up when people
are dead. Drumming up some business?" he said, referring to the
funeral parlor my ex and I co-owned together.

Officer Reed stood behind Joe and coughed. I actually felt
sorry for Reed. He was new to the force and was going to be a good
cop, in spite of having to tag along with Peters.

"Sandy, I mean Joe, I was out walking the dogs when Aaron
and I came upon this poor fellow. Shouldn't we do something to get
the pumpkin off him?"

Joe turned to Officer Reed. "I don't think he's going anywhere. Reed, call the station and get forensics out here. Tell them we need the medical examiner, too."

At that moment, Hank's Jeep pulled up to the curb. He slammed on the brakes, turned off the car, then flung open the door and raced over to me. Nina and Porkchop jumped at his legs, excited to see him. Hank folded me into his arms then placed me at arm's length. "Are you all right?" he asked, running his strong hands up and down my arms. His hands sent a calming warmth through the sweater I wore under my down vest.

I pointed to the pumpkin.

Hanks's crystal-blue eyes widened. "What's that?

Peters overheard his question and walked over to us. His unibrow arched upwards. "It looks like your girlfriend here is involved in another…what I'd call suspicious death."

Aaron stepped forward. "Hank, that's not what happened. Sam and I didn't do a thing. I was out jogging and ran into Sam walking the dogs." Aaron glanced down at the pups, who sat at our feet looking from one of us to the other as if watching a tennis match. "We were on the other side of the park when we heard people talking loudly. It sounded like they were arguing. We heard someone shout, so we ran over to see what was happening."

Hank frowned at his brother then turned his gaze on me. "Saaammm," Hank drawled out.

I looked down at my shoes and scuffed them on the sidewalk. I felt like I was back in grade school being scolded by my teacher. Not that I ever was. I was too afraid of disappointing my parents to be one of the school's troublemakers. "I didn't go looking for a dead person. He just happened to be there. Aaron and I went to do our civic duty and help a person in distress."

Hank pulled me up against him. "What am I going to do with you?" he whispered into my curly hair.

"Love me," I whispered back.

He hugged me a little tighter. "Oh, I do. I do."

"I hate to break up this love fest, but the EMTs have arrived. Even though there's not much for them to do. Doc Cordone is here, too."

Joe's sharp words snapped me back to the present. I stepped out of Hank's arms.

"What do we have here?" Doc Cordone rocked hack on the heels of his scuffed brown leather oxfords and looked over his half-glasses at us. His wispy gray hair stirred in the slight breeze blowing through the park, rustling the leaves of the oak and maple trees.

"Not sure yet, Doc, but we have a victim under the pumpkin," Hank said.

"Under the pumpkin, huh? Let me take a look. It's what I'm here for, right?" Doc chuckled.

Dark humor. I couldn't blame Doc Cordone for seeing a bit of humor in the situation. Sometimes I thought it was what kept people involved in gruesome situations sane.

Doc pointed to the pumpkin. "We'll need to get this pumpkin off the poor fellow first."

The crime scene technicians had been busy snapping photos of the area.

"You guys ready for us to move the pumpkin?" Hank asked a sandy-haired officer who held a camera in his hands.

"I've got what I need," the officer replied to Hank's question. "We'll concentrate on the surrounding area now."

"Scooter Dickenson said it weighed over two thousand pounds," I said as I watched the guys attempt to roll the pumpkin off the poor fellow lying underneath.

"No, sh… I mean no kidding. It's no wonder this fellow didn't survive this pumpkin landing on him." Joe swiped a hand over his forehead to brush away the sweat running into his eyes.

"Okay, one last shove and I think we've got it," Hank said as he dug his feet into the ground and pushed with his shoulder.

A loud *umph* was heard from all the men as they pushed with all of their might.

"Watch it," Hank shouted as the pumpkin rolled off the body and towards two EMTs standing beside their ambulance. They jumped out of the way as the pumpkin came to a stop inches from their vehicle.

"Sam, don't look. This isn't a pretty sight," Hank said.

My morbid curiosity won out as I stared at the gentleman lying on the ground. I started to sway, and bile rose into my mouth. While he wasn't the nicest man I had known and for such a brief time—really for only a matter of hours—Edgar Jensen didn't deserve to die like this…squashed by a prize-winning pumpkin.

My thoughts drifted to his wife, Carol. They looked to be having a rough time, matrimony wise, today, from the arguments I witnessed at the fair. It didn't help his making a pass at Joy either, but what couple didn't have disagreements? Hopefully, they made up before this accident happened. It would be horrible to think he died and they were still at odds with each other. My next thought drifted to how the pumpkin could have landed on him in the first place. True, earlier in the day Hank had noticed it wasn't secured very well to the flatbed of the truck, but what could have caused it to roll off the truck and onto him? Did he accidentally bump into the flatbed? My eyes widened. Or did someone deliberately push him against the truck, and it set the pumpkin in motion? I glanced over to Aaron. Did he kill Edgar? He did say he'd run past two people while jogging. We had heard arguing and a shout while we stood together talking, but what if it wasn't connected to Edgar's death? And what if Aaron had approached me from the opposite direction of the commotion? Maybe he had doubled around, making it look like he came from a different way? Could Aaron have killed Edgar? He'd said he was still upset about the man making a pass at Joy. My heart sank at these thoughts.

CHAPTER TWENTY

My eyes snapped open when Candie poked me in the ribs. "What's that for?" I asked, rubbing my side. I had been lost in my thoughts of Friday night and the events of yesterday, especially finding Edgar Jensen's body. I glanced around the café. Franny Goodway had decorated it in a 50s theme. The café wasn't anything fancy. Booths hugged three of its glossy white walls. A jukebox sat at the end of each table, but don't go flipping through the playlist looking for what's new on the hit parade. Franny's selection ran to the hits of the 50s, 60s, and 70s, which was fine with me. A checkerboard pattern of black and white tiles covered the floor. Even though my cousin was now married, we still met here on Sunday mornings. This was a habit we started over fifteen years ago when Candie moved north. I'd told Candie to invite Mark along, but she said this was a special time for us and no man was allowed.

"You were nodding off in church earlier, too. Did you have a late night with Hank?" Candie wiggled her eyebrows at me.

"I spent most of the evening with Hank, but it wasn't snuggling on my sofa." I placed a hand over my mouth to stifle a yawn. I hadn't told my cousin yet about my walk in the park or Edgar Jensen being killed by a pumpkin. It was too late when I got home, after midnight, and when she picked me up in Precious, her '73 baby blue Mustang convertible, this morning, I wasn't up to relating what had taken place in the park.

"By the way, what does Dixie think of Cuddles?" I wondered if Candie's cat took to the new dog better than she had to Porkchop. When Porkchop and I visited his Aunt Candie, the two animals kept their distance, giving each other plenty of room with only the occasional growl or hiss.

"Weeelll, we had a few moments when I first introduced Dixie to Cuddles. Some fur did stand on end with both pets. But then Cuddles, the sweetheart, did the cutest thing. He walked over to

Dixie's toy basket, plucked up her favorite mouse toy, and brought it over to Dixie and laid the toy at her feet. Dixie licked her toy then licked one of Cuddles's paws. I think she was saying thank you to Cuddles."

"That was really sweet of both Cuddles and Dixie. It sounds like you have the perfect match with those two." I took a sip of the coffee our waitress had delivered when she came to take our breakfast order. Unfortunately, because my blood pressure was on the rise, it was decaf. I doubted my java would do much to energize me.

I looked around the café. A number of church services were ending, so it was quickly filling up. Since I'd lived most of my life in Wings Falls, I knew a number of the diners as they walked in. I nodded at Doc Sorenson, our local veterinarian, sitting on a stool at the counter lining the far wall of the café. He saw to the pet needs of most of Wings Falls. A stack of flapjacks sat on a plate in front of him.

Candie tapped the faded red Formica tabletop with her equally red fingernails to get my attention. "You haven't answered my question."

I turned back to her. "What question?"

Candie rolled her eyes. "If you didn't spend the evening with Hank, something kept you up late. What was it?"

"Here you go, ladies. I hope you enjoy your breakfast."

I scootched back in my seat so the waitress, a new one to Sweetie Pie's, could place my breakfast in front of me. Her name tag read Dottie. She was older than most of the other waitresses. If I were to guess, I'd say in her late forties.

I pointed to my Sunday usual—a bowl of grits with a pat of butter floating on top. "Thank you, Dottie."

"Sure enough, ladies. Take your time. Would you like me to top off your coffee?" she asked, pointing towards our half-empty mugs.

"Sugar, I'd love some." Candie scooted her mug towards Dottie.

"Be right back," Dottie said and turned towards a counter holding the coffee machines.

I placed my spoon in my bowl of grits. As I stirred the melting butter into my grits, my hand shook. Bile rose into my mouth and my stomach churned over. Sweat beaded my forehead. "Jell-O," I whispered.

Candie reached across the table and clasped my hand. "Darling, what's the matter? You look positively green. Are you coming down with something?"

"Jell-O. Sandy said he looked like Jell-O lying on the ground all squished."

A frown creased Candie's forehead. "What are you talking about? Did you want a bowl of Jell-O instead of your grits? I'll call Dottie back and order you some if you'd like. What flavor do you want? Lime? Strawberry?"

I placed a hand over my mouth and stood up. I made a dash to the ladies' room. Candie was on my heels, concern etched her face.

I pushed open the door and ran to the nearest stall, where I emptied whatever was in my stomach into the porcelain god.

I could hear Candie ripping a piece of paper towel out of the dispenser next to the sinks and running the faucet. "Sweetie, place this across your forehead. If you wait a second, I'll go fetch a glass of water to rinse your mouth out."

I nodded, and with a shaking hand, I reached back and took the paper towel from her. I swiped it across my forehead. The cool water felt good. The door to the bathroom swished shut behind me as Candie left to get the water. I pushed myself to my feet. My legs wobbled, but I managed to make it to a folding chair sitting in the corner of the room. I lowered myself, closed my eyes, and leaned my head back against the wall. Bad idea. Behind my closed eyes danced visions of Edgar Jensen lying on the ground.

Within a few minutes, Candie was back. "Here, drink this." She placed the glass of cold water in my shaking hand.

"Thank you," I said with a tremulous smile.

Candie stood with her hands on her hips. She was in full protective mode. "Now tell me what has gotten you so upset. Did Hank do something?"

"I wish it were that simple," I said and proceeded to tell her about how Aaron and I found Edgar Jensen under a pumpkin.

"He was really killed by Scooter Dickenson's pumpkin? Woo-wee. What a way to meet your maker."

I nodded. "I can think of easier ways to enter heaven, if that's where he went. Although, he may be in the very hot place below if all the people he's angered had anything to say about it."

"You're right. He did upset a few folks. Remember the nasty comment he made to Joy yesterday and how Aaron responded? Although, I think any beau would have gotten upset if someone said anything as crude as he did to their gal."

I smiled. Candie, ever the romantic, would see the righteousness in defending a loved one. It was probably why she was so good at writing her romance novels.

"Aaron wasn't the only one upset yesterday with Edgar. I saw Joe Peters arguing with him over the loan he wants to help his wife, Portia, open her store, and then there's Clint Higgins, who has to purchase a new stove and refrigerator for his restaurant, Franny who needs money to help Joy with her college expenses, and Bill Collins and his sons from The Round Up, who have the health department breathing down their necks to make repairs to their restaurant or they are going to be shut down. Finally, and not least of all, Edgar's wife was arguing with him at the fair."

Candie shook her head. "My, oh my, that is a long list of people who wanted to see him roast down below."

"Yes, but someone wanted to see him roast more than anyone else. The one I'm most worried about is Aaron. He was really angry with Edgar yesterday. So he has a motive, even though I know he didn't do it. Still, if there's enough evidence, even circumstantial, it might be enough for a judge. I can't imagine what it would do to Hank if he had to arrest his brother for Edgar's murder." I wondered who else was on the list of suspects. That pumpkin needed a little help from someone to fall off of Scooter's truck, but I knew in my heart it wasn't Aaron and would do what I could to help prove him innocent.

CHAPTER TWENTY-ONE

———

"I think I'm ready to go back to our booth now." I grabbed on to the edge of the porcelain sink next to me and pulled myself up. My legs were still a bit wobbly.

Candie put her arm through mine to steady me. "Are you sure? We can skip breakfast and I'll drop you off at home. Mark's busy down at his campaign headquarters, so he won't be home. We can spend some time together. I'm trying to lie a little low these last few weeks of his campaign. I don't want anyone bringing up the nastiness that happened this past summer."

I cringed thinking about that horrible episode in her life right before hers and Mark's wedding and his primary election for mayor. Her first fiancé was murdered in her house, her bedroom to be more specific, and a racy picture of her was leaked to the press and made front page headlines in the town's newspapers. Luckily, the murderer was caught and the public was kind enough to dismiss the picture as a folly from her youth. Mark won the primary by a landslide.

I squeezed Candie's arm. "Now don't you go worrying about such things. After the election, Wings Falls will welcome you again as their First Lady with open arms."

Candie came to an abrupt halt by one of the mirrors on the wall over the sinks. She pushed back her auburn curls and turned her face from side to side. "Oh my, I hadn't thought of my position as Mark's wife. I really am Wings Falls' First Lady. I better get over to Shear Satisfaction and have Lizzie give me a trim."

I laughed. My cousin was totally unaware of her natural beauty. "You don't have to worry about your hair or anything else. What are you doing?"

Candie stood in front of the mirror waving her hand back and forth like the Queen of England riding down the streets of London in her royal carriage. "Practicing my wave for when Mark and I greet the citizens of Wings Falls."

I poked her in the ribs and laughed. "Come on, Your Highness. Our breakfast awaits and is getting colder by the minute."

We linked our arms together and, laughing, exited the ladies' room to a few quizzical stares from the diners we passed on the way to our table.

When I sat back down at our table, I stared at my now cold bowl of grits. At least the cold lump of cereal no longer reminded me of Jell-O. I motioned Dottie over to our table.

"What can I do for you ladies? More coffee?" she asked, hovering a steaming pot over my half-empty mug.

I waved a hand over my bowl of grits. "That would be great, but can you warm up our breakfasts in the microwave? I needed to visit the ladies' room, and they got a little cold."

"Honey, no problem. Let me grab a tray and I'll scoop them up and nuke them." Dottie was back in a few seconds and placed our breakfast on a large brown serving tray.

I leaned over the table towards Candie. "Do you want to stop by Discount World on the way home? I hear they are having a storewide sale, and I'd like to check it out."

Candie nodded. "Oh, that sounds like a wonderful idea. I can check out their doggie outfits and see if they have something for Cuddles. His wardrobe is so lacking right now. I want him to be the best dressed doggie in Wings Falls."

I almost spit out the coffee I was drinking. I swallowed hard and coughed. "Candie, you are going to spoil him rotten. What will Dixie think?"

Candie waved away my comment. "Dixie? I'll buy her a catnip mouse and she'll be in heaven. Cats don't take to all the fussing like a pup does."

I had to agree with her. I dressed up Porkchop when the mood struck me, and he never gave me any problems with it, but most of the time, he went au natural.

"Here you go, ladies. I hope you enjoy your warmed-over breakfast." Dottie placed out meals in front of us. This time I wasn't going to let the vision of Edgar lying on the ground interfere with my enjoyment of Franny's wonderful bowl of grits.

* * *

Discount World's parking lot was jam packed. All of Wings Falls must have received their sale flyer in the mail.

"There, over there." I pointed out the window at a car backing out of a parking space.

Candie followed my directions, and Precious shot forward to fill the empty space.

"We were lucky," Candie said as we exited her car.

"Yeah. We could have been circling the parking lot forever looking for a space," I said, grabbing a shopping cart from the nearest corral.

We entered the store, to be greeted by an employee handing us a sales flyer and wishing us happy bargain hunting. I gazed around the store, amazed at the number of people shopping, although I shouldn't have been surprised if the number of cars in the parking lot was any indication of what was inside.

Candie's head swiveled around the store. "It looks like Black Friday."

I nodded. "I wonder if the people taking advantage of the bargains are doing some Christmas shopping early."

"I'd better get over to the pet department before everything is sold out," Candie said, turning her cart in that direction.

"Hey, wait for me," I shouted after her. She was on a mission, and nothing was going to stop her. I hoped no one got in her way. Things could get ugly if they did.

I trailed after Candie, repeating, "Excuse me," as I made my way through the crowd of people, their carts full of everything from jeans to electronics. I had nothing specific in mind I wanted to purchase. I was going to just let an item jump out at me. I could do some pre-Christmas shopping like everyone else.

"Sam, Sam over here."

I craned my neck to see where Candie was calling from. Sure enough, it was the pet department, and she was waving a doggie outfit at me. I steered my shopping cart towards her, weaving in and out of the packed aisles. My eyes widened as I scanned the contents of her shopping cart. "Have you left anything for the other pet lovers to buy?"

Candie frowned at me, clearly not happy with my question. "I've gotten a few essentials for Cuddles. Especially since the weather is getting colder. I can't have him shivering his tiny little butt off." Candie held up a baby blue poofy-hooded doggie coat and a matching pair of snow booties. Three hooded sweatshirts and a raincoat with matching rain boots lay in the bottom of the cart.

I picked up a cardboard hanger that held four doggie scarves and raised an eyebrow at her. "What are these for?"

Candie snatched them out of my hand. "Cuddles can't go visiting unless he's properly dressed."

I rolled my eyes and mumbled, "Porkchop must feel positively naked when we leave the house."

As a shopper's cart bumped into me, I said, "Oops." I caught myself before I stumbled into Candie. I turned to give the careless shopper the evil eye and a snide remark but stopped before I put my foot in my mouth. This woman still intimidated me decades later.

CHAPTER TWENTY-TWO

————

"Oh hi, Portia. Shopping for bargains?" I did a mental palm plant. Duh. Of course she was. Why else would she be here?

Portia flicked back a stand of long, over-bleached blonde hair from her round face. "Yes. I need to buy office supplies for the new consignment shop I'm going to open up. You know, receipt books, sales tags, paper, pens…"

"Hank mentioned Joe was talking at the station about your new adventure. You are going to open up a used clothing store," I said.

Portia's chin shot up. She gripped the handle of her shopping cart so hard her knuckles turned white. "It is not a used clothing store. A person will be able to purchase upcycled treasures from me, an article of clothing that has been gently worn. I will only have the finest fashion finds to choose from in my boutique."

Whoa. I took a step back from the vehemence in her voice. "I'm sorry. Hank only repeated what Joe told him."

"The knucklehead. If I've told him once about my store, I've told him a dozen times, but does he listen to me? No. He's too busy watching his sports shows when he comes home from work."

I glanced over at Candie and shrugged my shoulders. Obviously, all was not smooth sailing in the Peters' household. Candie responded with a nod of her head. She had received my silent message.

"What's the name of your new store, and where are you opening up?" In spite of its being a small community, Wings Falls' businesses were thriving. I did a mental walk down the streets of the town and could envision only a few vacant storefronts, and those weren't situated in an area of high traffic flow. I might not be a business wizard, but even I knew it would be tough to make a success of a business in that part of town.

Portia's already plump chest puffed up even more. Gone was her petite high school cheerleader figure. I mentally did a high-five at my semi-maintaining a decent physique even though my gym visits were hit or miss, some weeks mostly miss.

"The name of my business is Top Drawer Consignments. You know, top drawer as in only the best. I got a deal of a lease on a storefront on South Street."

I bit my tongue. South Street was an area badly in need of sprucing up. Most towns suffered from a street or two that weren't the most desirable, and South Street was that street in Wings Falls. Mark had petitioned Albany for funds to help in revitalizing it, but with no luck so far. Hopefully, after he won the election next month, he would have more success wrangling the money from the powers-that-be in the capital.

"Umm, so you got the bank loan you need for opening your store? I heard people were having a bit of a problem dealing with Edgar Jensen at the Wings Falls National Bank."

Portia's face turned purple with rage. I was afraid she was about to have a stroke. "That evil man. I'm glad he's dead. What he's put me through, I would have gladly pushed the pumpkin on him and danced on it, too. He would grant me a loan only if I paid his 'special fees.'" Her fingers wiggled air quotes around the words *special fees*. "I'm sorry I wasn't there to clap when it happened."

"Do you think she's happy Edgar is dead?" Candie mumbled out of the side of her mouth.

"Maybe a wee bit," I returned. Maybe she knew about Edgar's passing before Joe told her. Could she have been in the park when he was killed? Maybe she was the one who killed him. Was she the one zooming away in her car?

"So, Joe told you about Edgar's passing? It certainly wasn't a pleasant way to die," I said. "Since Joe was working Saturday night, were you home alone?"

Portia frowned at my question. "Why do you ask? I'm often alone since he works odd hours. You should know that, what with you dating Hank."

"Umm, yes, I was just concerned since there seems to be another murderer on the loose in Wings Falls."

Portia's face color returned to a healthier pink. "If you must know I was home, busy going over the inventory I have for my new store, when Joe called me about Edgar's murder. He also said you phoned in the 9-1-1 call. You certainly show up at a lot of unexplained deaths. Back in school, instead of calling you Sam the Nerd, your nickname should have been Sam the Death Magnet."

I cringed at the mention of the taunt she used when we were in high school together. The years hadn't changed Portia's catty ways. "Yes, it is unfortunate I happen to stumble upon murder victims, but at least I've been successful in solving these cases that seem to stump your husband."

A big smile spread across Candie's face. "You go, girlfriend."

"Well. Umm, I'd better finish my shopping. I've got a ton of work to do before my grand opening," Portia started to back her shopping cart away from us.

"So, did you get the loan you need to open you store?" I asked before she could escape.

"Not yet, but with a new loan officer, I'm sure it will be no problem." Portia smiled and made a quick exit down the aisle, barely missing bumping into an older woman's cart. The woman stood next to a display of lingerie, trying to decide between bikini underwear or hip hugger briefs. I tried to envision Gladys in a pair of bikini panties. I shook my head and tried to erase the image from my brain.

Candie pushed her cart next to me. "She seems mighty happy Edgar is dead. Could she have killed him so the bank would hire a new loan officer and be a shoo-in for granting her loan?"

I nodded. "It certainly is a possibility. Portia could have been the person in the park arguing with Edgar. She could have sped home and been there when Joe called her. She certainly has a lot to gain with him dead. Like you said, she'd get the loan and not have to worry about losing her home. But it could also be a possibility for a few other people."

As we passed the older woman, Candie leaned over and pointed to the bikinis. "The hot pink ones, for sure."

The woman turned to Candie. "Thank you. You've helped me make up my mind."

I started to laugh and couldn't stop. "You're an original, Candie." I swiped at the tears rolling down my cheeks.

Candie looked at me with a picture of innocence on her face. "What are you talking about? I was only helping the poor woman with her decision."

"Come on, let's get on with our shopping. I need to go home and feed Porkchop and Nina."

Candie nodded. "Yes, and I can't wait to show Cuddles all the new outfits I bought him."

* * *

"Here, hand me your purchases. I'll place them in the back seat." I reached over and grabbed Candie's overflowing bags from her. At the rate she was buying outfits for Cuddles, Candie would accomplish her mission of making him the best-dressed pup in Wings Falls before the end of the week. I flipped up Precious's back seat and placed the shopping bags on the seat. They sat next to my meager purchase of laundry soap and a pair of jeans I nabbed on sale.

After I deposited the bags, I settled into the car's white leather seat beside Candie. I latched my seat belt then swiveled towards my cousin. "You know, Portia isn't the only one to mention Edgar charging his clients some kind of fee to guarantee them a bank loan. Franny referred to such a fee at the Taste of Wings Falls yesterday."

Candie placed the key in the car's ignition. Precious roared to life. For being an older car, she still had a lot of life left in her. "Clint Higgins and Bob Collins also needed money to keep their restaurants running. Do you think Edgar was charging them an extra fee, too? Would they have been so desperate for money to kill him?"

I shrugged my shoulders. "That might be the fifty-million-dollar question."

A car horn blared behind us. Because of Discount World's sale, parking places were at a premium. Candie shook her fist at the horn blower. She shifted the car into reverse and started to back out of the space.

I glanced out my window to see who the impatient person was, and my mouth dropped open. I tugged on the sleeve of Candie's sweater. "Candie, look. Look who is driving that car."

CHAPTER TWENTY-THREE

———

Candie's foot stomped on the brakes. "Heavens to Betsy! You about scared the spit out of me." She craned her neck to look over the back seat. "Oh, my. I see what you mean. She doesn't exactly look like the grieving widow, does she? Why is she driving such a rattletrap of a car? You'd think with the position her husband held at the bank, she'd be sitting behind the wheel of a brand-new, high-end car. You know, a Lexus or a BMW."

"Who knows. Maybe an expensive car isn't high on her priority list. But, no, she doesn't look like she's shedding any tears over Edgar's demise. Would you be at Discount World, shopping for bargains, the day after your husband died?"

"I'd be prostrate on my big ol' bed if something happened to my Mark. I don't know if I'd ever be able to get up. Well, maybe to tend to my Dixie and Cuddles, but then I'd have to go right back to my bed."

That "big ol' bed" my cousin was referring to was a huge, and I mean huge, antique Victorian-style bed with a headboard that reached almost to the ceiling of her bedroom. I'd say this for those strait-laced folks from the turn of the nineteenth century… They sure knew how to slumber in style.

"Maybe she wants to buy some widow's weeds and check out what Discount World has on sale."

I frowned at Candie. "Do you really think that's why Carol Jensen is here?"

Carol leaned on her car horn again. The heads of fellow shoppers passing by turned towards us.

"Come on. Let's get out of here before the store's security comes out to investigate what all the fuss is about."

"All right. All right. I'm going." Candie placed Precious in reverse and continued out of the parking space. As she passed Carol, she waggled her ringed fingers at her and stuck her tongue out.

"Candie! Stop that." I swatted at her arm.

"What?" Candie replied with a look of childhood innocence on her face.

"You know darn well what I'm referring to. Be kind. She lost her husband yesterday."

Candie tapped the steering wheel with her ruby-red fingernails. "You know who the main suspect in a person's death usually is?"

I looked at my cell phone to see if I had received any text messages from Hank. I hadn't heard from him since yesterday, other than a brief message I received this morning when I woke up—*I love you! I'll try to stop by tonight. Give Porkchop and Nina a scratch for me.* His text had warmed me all through Mass. It had pushed aside any disturbing thoughts of what happened last night. "No, who?"

Candie glanced over at me. We were stopped at a red light. "The spouse."

My mouth dropped open. My curls bounced about my shoulders as I shook my head. "You mean Carol? But she's so tiny. Nah, she couldn't have knocked the huge pumpkin on Edgar."

The light turned green, and we moved forward.

"Don't you remember? The pumpkin had a pretty good wobble to it. Hank even mentioned it to Scooter Dickenson. He asked him to secure the pumpkin better on his flatbed. What if Scooter never got around to following Hank's request?"

I sat silently in my seat, mulling over what Candie had said. *What if Scooter hadn't secured the pumpkin on his truck better? It did have a pretty good wobble. Could the voices Aaron and I heard arguing in the park been Carol's and Edgar's? Could she have shoved Edgar and caused the pumpkin to fall on him?*

"Here you are, home safe and sound, and lookee who is here to greet you!"

My brain snapped back to the present. My heart did a double beat, and warmth spread through my body. A smile curved my lips at the sight of a Jeep sitting in my driveway. A Jeep belonging to one hunky detective. "Hank," I whispered.

"Yep, it looks like the love of your life has come to pay a visit. Stop wasting time and go welcome him—and with a proper greeting, if you know what I mean."

Now heat rushed up my neck and into my face. Yep, I knew what kind of greeting Candie meant. I grabbed the door handle and flung open the door, reached into the back seat for my packages, and then raced up my drive.

"Goodbye to you, too," Candie laughed out the passenger-side window.

I waggled my fingers over my shoulder in response.

I was on a mission. A mission to throw my arms around Hank and never let him go. "Hank!" I called out when I opened the front door. I scanned the room but didn't see him. Where could he be? "Hank!" I repeated, tossing my bags onto the living room sofa. Still no response. Then I noticed Nina and Porkchop hadn't greeted me when I entered the house, either. It dawned on me where they could be. My darling boyfriend must have the doggies out back. I hurried through the kitchen and out the back door. What greeted me warmed my heart. Hank stood in the middle of my backyard playing fetch with the dogs, throwing a tennis ball and watching as Nina and Porkchop tried to beat each other to it. The dogs barked and yipped as they ran across my leaf-covered lawn.

Hank had his back to me, so he hadn't noticed I was here yet. I tiptoed over to him and hugged him from behind. He jumped at my touch.

"Geez, you scared me," he said, turning in my embrace.

I laughed. "You're the second person I've done that to today."

Hank frowned at me. "What? Hugged someone from behind? I don't know if I like that."

I reached up and pushed back the wayward brown curl of his with a mind of its own that insisted on falling onto his forehead. "No, silly. Scared someone. Guess I need a different approach."

Hank returned my hug and leaned down and kissed me. It was a good thing he held on to me, as I thought my knees would buckle. "So, who was the lucky person you scared out of their wits?"

Porkchop and Nina had become aware of my presence and were now jumping up on my legs to get my attention. I leaned down and petted both of their heads, but this didn't seem to quiet their excitement at my being home. "Let's go inside and get them a treat so they will settle down. Then I'll tell you about Candie's and my trip to Discount World." I glanced at both dogs, whose rear ends wagged back and forth with excitement. It warmed my heart seeing their unconditional love for me. Which I returned to them but without the rear end wagging. "Treat?" With the mention of that magic word, both dogs raced to the back door. I laughed. "So much for being excited to see me."

Hank raised my hand to his lips and placed a tender kiss on the palm. "I'm *very* excited to see you."

A shiver of delight raced through me. "I feel the same way. Now, let's get the dogs settled, and I'll tell you about my shopping expedition with Candie."

The dogs were snuggled together on a rug before my fireplace. Hank had built a fire, and I was curled up next to him on the sofa. He was drinking a Trail's Head beer while I sipped on a glass of Riesling. If only all my nights could be like this.

"So, who else did you scare the wits out of today?" Hank asked as he ran his fingers through my hair.

"Candie." I leaned into his hand and let the magic of his fingers relax me.

"How so?" he asked, leaning down and kissing the top of my head.

I related to him Candie's and my encounter with Carol Jensen in the parking lot then included our meeting Portia in the store.

"Do you think Portia or possibly Joe Peters could have killed Edgar?" I asked.

I felt Hank's body stiffen. He sat up straighter on the sofa. "Sam, don't let your animosity towards Joe prejudice your judgment. He's a good cop. Overzealous sometimes, but he is still a good cop."

I turned towards him. "Hank, Joe and I may not be the best buds, but I'm keeping an open mind in Edgar's death."

Hank raised one of his well-shaped eyebrows at me. Gone was the coziness I felt a few moments before.

I peered over the rim of my wineglass. "Are you keeping an open mind where your brother is concerned in this matter? Just because he got in trouble when he was younger doesn't mean he killed Edgar."

Hank rose from the sofa. "I think it's time Nina and I called it a night. Come here, girl."

Drat. I could have smacked myself on the forehead. When would I ever learn to bite my tongue before I speak? I looked up at Hank with pleading eyes. "I'm sorry, Hank. I didn't mean to bring up Aaron's name."

Hank nodded and walked towards the front door with Nina waddling behind him.

CHAPTER TWENTY-FOUR

———

Porkchop jumped up on the sofa next to me. I ran my hand over the cushion Hank had vacated. It still held the warmth of his body. Tears streamed down my face. Porkchop nuzzled his head onto my lap. "Porkie, when will I ever learn to think before I speak?" My pup gazed up at me with his chocolate-brown eyes then licked my hand.

* * *

"Phew. The wind is strong enough to knock a person over." Gladys poked her head into The Ewe and Me. I jumped out of my seat to grab the door before it swung back and slapped her in the rear and struggled to hide my smile. With all the wind today, Gladys's orange-dyed curls hadn't moved an inch. She must have super hair sprayed them this morning. I held out my hand to grab her oversize tan canvas bag. It was stuffed with her hooking frame, pattern, wool, and all the goodies needed to work on her rug.

She swatted at my hand. "I can handle this. What do you think I am, an old lady?"

"Well, you're no spring chicken," Helen Garber shouted from the end of the table we were sitting around for our Monday morning gathering of hookers.

Gladys plunked her bag on the table then placed her hands on her thin hips. She squinted her eyes and gave Helen a death-ray stare. "You've got nerve saying I'm no spring chicken, you old bird."

Helen opened her mouth to respond, but Lucy Foster, The Ewe's owner, stepped forward and said, "Anyone for a cup of coffee? Ralph stopped by Sweetie Pie's earlier and picked up some of Franny's cinnamon buns." Ralph was Lucy's husband and right-hand man at The Ewe. While he didn't hook, that wasn't to say a number of men don't rug hook. However, it still remained a female-dominated hobby. Ralph, a retired shop teacher, made sure The Ewe ran smoothly—helping at the checkout counter when Lucy was busy with customers, straightening shelves, seeing to any repairs in need of fixing, and most importantly of all—according to Porkchop—making sure there were doggie treats on hand when my Porkie accompanied me to The Ewe. In his world, my precious pup considered himself the official shop dog. He might allow other dogs, such as his friend Hana, to attend our weekly hooking sessions, but he thought of himself as the Top Dog.

Candie raised her hand. "Honey, coffee and a cinnamon bun would hit the spot right about now. It's been some weekend."

"Tell me about it," Gladys said with a huff as she pulled her equipment out of her bag. She shook out a partially completed rug featuring two orange roosters. They matched the color of her hair.

Anita Plum looked up from her rug. "I heard there was an incident at the Taste on Saturday and a number of people became ill. Were you one of them, Gladys?"

Gladys pulled a baggy red sweater about her scrawny body. "I sure was. Weren't you there?"

Anita, the mother of twin teenage girls, shook her head. "No, my girls had basketball games on Saturday. They're on a traveling team. It takes up most of our weekends. But they love the sport, and who knows, maybe, fingers crossed, a college will see them and offer the girls a scholarship."

"It certainly would be fabulous since you'd have the two of them attending college at the same time."

Heads nodded around the table in agreement with me.

Including myself, there were eleven of us gathered around the long oak table in The Ewe this morning. Porkchop reclined under the table at my feet, chewing on a rawhide bone. Hana, Patsy Ikeda's dog, did the same. I gazed around the room, taking in the cubies and antique furniture stuffed with pieces of wool in all colors of the rainbow. My eyes settled on Marybeth Higgins, who sat quietly hooking at the end of the table. I was surprised to see her here, since her brother, Clint, was on my list of possible suspects in Edgar Jensen's death and the tainting of the barbeque served at the Taste on Saturday.

Lucy walked out of the back room pushing a cart with a coffeepot, mugs, and a tray full of fresh cinnamon buns. The smell of which had my mouth watering. One of the pastries I enjoyed most from Sweetie Pie's were Franny's cinnamon buns. It was impossible to eat just one.

Lucy parked the cart in the corner of the room. "Here you go, ladies. Enjoy."

Gladys led the line as we all filled a mug with coffee and placed a bun on a paper plate Lucy provided. Porkchop got up from his resting place and budged into the line.

I bent and grabbed on to his collar. "I'm sorry, Porkie. I know the pastries smell delicious, but they aren't for little doggies like you. I shouldn't even indulge." I could almost feel my black yoga pants tightening around my waist as I sniffed their aroma. Porkchop whined. My heart went out to him, but it was bad enough when I ate pizza and I gave him my crust to munch on.

When we settled back down at the table, I noticed Helen staring at her cinnamon bun. This was unusual for her, as she was never one to pass up a sweet.

"Something wrong?" I asked.

Helen looked over the rim of her bright orange glasses at me. "I heard the police suspect the people at the Taste got sick eating barbeque from one of the vendors. Since Franny was one of them, do you think this is safe to eat? What if she's gone crazy and is trying to poison all of Wings Falls? You know, like a mass murderer."

"Helen!" Candie screeched. "You've said some pretty outrageous things in the past, but your statement tops them. We all know Franny, and she wouldn't hurt a fly. You should be ashamed of yourself." Having said that, Candie took a large bite of her bun.

I wanted to stand up and applaud my cousin. In fact, I did just that—clap my hands. I was afraid to rise. I didn't want to upend anyone's coffee if I bumped into the table when I stood.

Helen pushed up her at glasses that had slipped down her nose and puffed out her already large chest. "If it wasn't Franny's barbeque making fairgoers sick, then whose was it?"

I peeked at the end of the table over the rim of my mug. Marybeth looked as if she wanted to sink under the table. I sent her a smile and did a thumbs-up. She returned my smile and nodded her head. She looked Helen in the eye. "In case you didn't know, Clint was selling his pulled pork sandwiches at the fair, too."

Helen's mouth dropped open and started to stutter. "Well…what… Are you sure?"

This was one of the rare times I had seen her speechless.

Marybeth looked pointedly at Helen and slammed her coffee mug on the table. A few drops of coffee splashed out of the mug. "And if you were wondering, Bill Collins from The Round Up was also there selling his award-winning barbeque. The police took all of our trays of barbeque to send to a lab in Albany, and then they shut us down. The lab tests will prove we had nothing to do with people getting ill. " She grabbed her napkin and swiped at the droplets.

Helen picked up her napkin and twisted it in between her plump fingers. "Ummm, ummm, I didn't mean to insinuate anything."

"Yeah, that will be the day," Candie mumbled out the side of her mouth.

I sputtered and coughed on a mouthful of coffee I had tried to swallow.

"Love Me Tender" sang out from my designer purse choice of the day, a red Fendi. I fished in my purse for my phone and pulled it out of a mass of store receipts, my wallet, and one of those secure cases holding my credit cards. I was surprised to see the caller ID read Bob Spellman, my editor at Rolling Brook Press. My picture book, *Porkchop, the Wonder Dog,* was going to be released next month in time for the holiday sales. My hope and wish was for all good parents to buy a copy for their children.

I flipped it open, pushing aside my mass of curly brown hair. "Hi, Bob. What's up? What? Noooo." *How and why would someone want to pirate my book?*

CHAPTER TWENTY-FIVE

———

Heat rushed up my neck with anger. I gripped my phone so tightly my knuckles turned white. "How can someone do this? You say they have it listed online for free. How did they even get hold of a copy? I hope you fired him. Okay, I know you'll handle it. Thank you for letting me know." I snapped my phone closed and blew out a deep breath.

All the Loopy Ladies' eyes were trained on me. Embarrassed by my show of anger, I felt the red color of both rage and embarrassment showing on my face.

Candie placed her hand on mine. "Sugar, what happened to get you so upset? Is everything all right?"

The ladies sitting around the table added words of concern to Candie's.

I shook my head. "That was Bob Spellman, my editor for Porkchop's book." At the mention of his name, Porkchop lifted his head, but after realizing no more treats were coming his way, he returned to enjoying his rawhide bone.

Cookie Harrington looked up from her hooking. She was creating a rug with a train design for her nephews. "That's right. It comes out next month, doesn't it? I've preordered a copy for my brother's young boys. I'm going to give it to them as a Christmas present. Do you think Porkchop can autograph it for me?"

"We may have to delay the release date of my book so Mr. Spellman can straighten out this piracy mess we have on our hands."

Gasps and exclamations of surprise resounded in the room.

My heart warmed and my spirits rose at my friends' support for me and my dilemma. "Apparently, a young intern at Rolling Brook sent a copy of the cover of *Porkchop, the Wonder Dog,* to an internet site that pirates ebooks. Usually, those sites are a scam. They ask the person to sign up for some special offer then take a person's money, but the one ordering the book never sees it."

"Why would someone be so foolish to do such a thing?" Anita asked as she dug through a pile of wool strips sitting on the table before her.

"Money," Jane Burrows added. "The intern probably got paid by the site for getting them access to your cover, Sam. We are extra careful at the library when ordering books. There are only a few sites I allow my acquisitions person to order from. We can't take the chance of losing money by going to one of those bogus sites, no matter how good the book deal looks."

Candie patted my hand. "I'm sure Mr. Spellman will have this all worked out before your book is released."

I managed a faint smile for my cousin. "I certainly hope so. I worked hard to write my book and have been so excited about it. This puts a damper on things."

My coffee mug jumped as Candie slapped the table. "Samantha Reynolds Davies, now stop that! What would Memaw Parker say in a situation like this?"

I jutted out my chin. "We're Parkers and we can do anything!"

Candie pulled me into a hug. "That's right, and don't you forget it. Now let's get down to some serious hooking."

* * *

After Candie's pep talk, the morning flew by. Conversations about children and the happenings in the daily lives of the Loopy Ladies took center stage. No more talk about the fair, Edgar Jensen's demise, or my book troubles. We laughed when Roberta Holden told us a story her four-year-old grandson, Cody, invented. He was visiting Grandma and informed her he got his head stuck in the toilet and his dad had to pull him out. Apparently, her daughter and son-in-law were in the midst of trying to potty train their son. We all laughed until tears ran down our cheeks.

Before we knew it, we were calling it a day until we met again the following Monday. Since a number of the Loopy Ladies were retired or self-employed, we answered to our own schedules. But Cookie Harrington needed to head out to her job at the Wings Falls Animal Hospital, Susan Mayfield was due at her restaurant, Momma Mia's, and Marybeth Higgins's shift at the Wings Falls Hospital, where she was a nurse, would soon begin.

As we gathered up our hooking supplies, I grabbed the cart Lucy had served the coffee and cinnamon buns from. It was now loaded with empty mugs. I wheeled it into the dye room and placed the mugs into the stainless-steel sink, then filled the sink with soap and water.

"Here's a couple more for you."

I turned to see Marybeth holding out two more mugs. "Thanks. I guess I missed them."

Marybeth laughed. "Gladys wasn't quite finished with her coffee and wanted to make sure she got the very last drop."

I reached for the mugs. "That's our Gladys."

Should I or shouldn't I ask her? I had Marybeth's undivided attention, so why not go for it. "Marybeth, I heard Clint had some issues with Edgar Jensen."

Marybeth's face paled. One of the mugs slipped from her shaking hand and crashed to the floor. "Oh, look what I've done."

Had I struck a nerve, I wondered as I handed her some paper towels from the dispenser that hung over the sink. She bent and scooped up the broken pieces of mug then deposited them in the trash can under the sink.

"Where did you hear that?"

Now it was my turn to squirm. Marybeth was a friend. It wasn't easy asking her this kind of question. "Ummm. I think someone mentioned it at the fair on Saturday."

"It's no secret. Clint had to spend a lot of money renovating The Smiling Pig in order to open. Two things had to wait to be replaced, the stove and refrigerator. Unfortunately, Clint can't put off purchasing new ones any longer."

I turned to the sink and started to scrub the dirty mugs. Marybeth stood next to me with a towel to dry the mugs as I handed them to her. "So, he approached Edgar for a loan to make these purchases. I know they are quite expensive."

Marybeth nodded. Straight brown hair bounced on her shoulders. "Thousands. They cost thousands of dollars. He went to the Wings Falls National Bank and met with Edgar about obtaining a loan."

I swiped at the coffee stain in the bottom of a mug. "Edgar agreed to the loan?"

A sneer crossed Marybeth's face. "Oh, yeah. He agreed all right."

"So, what was the problem? Clint would get the money he needed for the appliances and all would be fine at The Smiling Pig."

Marybeth let out a bitter laugh. "He could get the loan if Clint agreed to paying a 'special fee' on top of the interest rate the bank charged."

I frowned. This wasn't the first time I'd heard of the special fee in order to secure a bank loan. What was it all about? How could Edgar get away with it? Was it because his father-in-law was president of the bank?

I handed Marybeth the last mug to dry and unplugged the drain. "Did Clint agree to these terms and get the loan?"

"No, he told Edgar what he thought of his 'special fee' then went to the Sandy Hill Savings and Loan and applied for a loan there."

Sandy Hill was the town neighboring Wings Falls. Like Wings Falls, it prided itself on its friendly, small-town atmosphere. I often went there to purchase my favorite chocolate cookies from Mandy Valentine, the owner of The Cookie Shop.

"Was he successful?" I asked as I ripped a wad of paper towel from the dispenser and wiped my hands dry.

Marybeth placed the last mug on the counter. "Yes, he was. The bank saw how well the restaurant is doing and felt it was a low-risk loan. The new stove and refrigerator were delivered last week."

Since Clint went to a different bank for his loan and didn't really have any dealings with Edgar, would this take him off my suspect list?

"People should mind their own business. They'd be a lot happier. But if you ask me, I'm not surprised at Edgar's death."

My head snapped up from arranging the mugs on a shelf above the sink. *What was that all about?*

CHAPTER TWENTY-SIX

———

Candie grasped her rug hooking bag in one hand and circled me with her free arm in a side-hug. "Mark is working, so I need to get home and tend to my Cuddles and Dixie."

"Are they still getting along?" Even after Dixie had seemed to accept Cuddles, I had wondered how Dixie would take to a canine addition to the family.

"Like they were besties for life. When I left, they were snuggled next to each other on the sofa."

I pushed the door of The Ewe open for her and laughed. "I guess miracles do happen."

She gave me a peck on the cheek. "Smartie pants. Call me later."

I waved and Porkchop yipped as she continued across the parking lot to Precious.

Porkchop and I were walking out to my car when Roberta Holden scooted up to me. "Sam, Clyde told me that you discovered Edgar Jensen's body."

My eyebrows rose at her knowing I was the one to find Edgar. Although, maybe I shouldn't have been. Her husband owned the town's most popular barber shop. It was also known as gossip central. If something happened in Wings Falls, it was certain to be the main topic of conversation of the fellows sitting in his barber chair. "How did he find out? He's not open today, is he?"

Roberta blushed. "Not usually, but he had an emergency haircut appointment this morning. One of his best clients was going on a blind date tonight and needed a trim. He wanted to impress the woman. Men! And they think we're vain."

Porkchop strained at his leash. "One minute, sweetie." I opened my car door, picked him up, and placed him on the front seat. He circled the seat then lay down. I turned back to Roberta. "Clyde's customer was correct. I was walking the dogs in the park and came upon Edgar. Unfortunately, he was dead."

Roberta bounced on the balls of her feet. "Ohh. Ohh. Can I quote you for the *Senior Chatter?"* She reached into her oversize handbag and drew out a pen and small tablet of paper.

I did an inward groan and raised my eyes towards heaven. *Why me, Lord?* I silently asked. "Don't you usually report on the town council meetings? Would this be appropriate for your column?" I really didn't want to be featured in any newspaper, whether it was small like the *Senior Chatter* or had a large circulation like the *Tribune.*

Roberta flipped open the pad of paper and poised her pen over it, waiting for me to give her an answer.

"Roberta, I really don't have anything to say about Saturday night. If you want any details, I'd suggest calling the Wings Falls Police Department. I'm sorry, but I need to get Porkchop home. It's past his lunchtime. He gets quite moody if I don't feed him on a strict schedule."

"I'm sorry. I didn't realize Porkchop has such a delicate constitution. I'll take your advice and call the police station." She thanked me then walked over to her car.

I congratulated myself as I opened the car's trunk and stowed my rug hooking gear. I had successfully dodged Roberta's questions. I wished her good luck getting any information out of the police, especially when it was an active investigation. I walked to the driver's side of the car, pulled open the door, and settled into my seat. I glanced over at Porkchop nestled in the seat next to me. He opened one eye, as if to acknowledge my presence, then closed it. I laughed. "How's that delicate constitution of yours, Porkchop? Let's get home and feed it." I placed the Bug in reverse and headed home.

* * *

I spent the rest of the day doing some much-needed cleaning of my home. I had been so busy preparing for the launch of *Porkchop, the Wonder Dog,* I had neglected the dusting and vacuuming. The kitchen floor needed a good mopping, too. Porkchop's paw prints were beginning to be the main design pattern. Who knew alerting the reading public of my forthcoming book would take so much of my time—setting up a social media platform, placing ads on book selling sites, shouting about it from rooftops? Well, maybe not the shouting from rooftops part, but at times, that's what I thought I was doing. So, dressed in my oldest sweatpants and sweatshirt—the pants with the holes in the knees and a sweatshirt decorated with paint down the front from trying to give a table a shabby chic look—I tied my hair back with an old purple scarf. Then I got set to do some serious damage to the built-up dirt and dust because my dust bunnies had morphed into dust elephants.

I had been dusting, vacuuming, and mopping like a crazy woman when I heard a knock at my front door. Porkchop, who was supervising my whirlwind activity, ran to the door, barking and wagging his tail. I glanced at the digital clock on my stove—seven o'clock. Who could it be? I suspected most people would be home right now, curled up on their sofas enjoying an after dinner glass of wine or cup of tea.

I had taken a break earlier from my cleaning and spoken to Candie. I'd tried to call Hank, but it went straight to his voice mail. I didn't know if he was busy with the case or still miffed at me.

I walked to the front door and peered out the peephole and frowned. Pink roses stared back at me. I flung open the door. Porkchop jumped with joy at the person gripping what appeared to be a dozen of the most beautiful pink roses.

Hank lowered the bouquet and gave me a crooked smile. That wayward brown curl of his rested on his forehead. "Can I come in?"

My lips lifted in a huge smile, and I reached up and brushed back the curl. "Of course. You don't have to ask."

"From the way I left last night, I didn't know how welcome I'd be." A Fred Flintstone tie lay loosely around his neck. His sport jacket hung open. He must have come straight from work.

"Come in." I stepped back to allow him to follow me into my living room.

As I walked past the mirror hanging in my entrance way, I gasped. I pulled the scarf off my head and swiped at the dirt smudges on my cheeks.

"Have a seat," I said, motioning towards the sofa.

Hank held out the beautiful roses. "These are for you. I'm sorry about the way I left last night."

I took the bouquet and sniffed the flowers. Their scent was intoxicating. "These are beautiful. Thank you. Let me fetch a vase for them. They are such a beautiful shade of pink."

"The lady at Blooms said the color pink stands for forgiveness. Are they working on you?"

I reached up into a kitchen cabinet and pulled down a crystal vase that had belonged to my Memaw Parker. "They've done the job," I said, filling the vase with water and arranging the roses in it. "Would you like a Trail's Head?" I called out from the kitchen.

"That would be great, if it's not a bother."

I opened the refrigerator door and pulled out his favorite beer. "Never a bother," I answered back. I reached in one more time for the bottle of Riesling I had chilling in the door of the refrigerator. When I returned to the living room with his beer and my glass of wine, my heart leapt into my throat. Hank sat on the edge of the sofa with his hands clasped between his knees, a look of utter sorrow on his handsome face. Porkchop sat at his feet, licking those strong hands. Hands that could give me such pleasure but now looked as tired and dejected as the rest of him.

CHAPTER TWENTY-SEVEN

I placed the drinks on the coffee table in front of the sofa then sat down next to Hank. I took his hands in mine and kissed them then pulled him to me in an embrace. He rested his head on my shoulder. I could feel tears wetting my sweatshirt. His body shook as I rubbed his back. This strong man whom I loved was wracked with pain, and I could guess the reason why—his baby brother Aaron.

After few moments of indulging in his grief, Hank sat up straight and scrubbed the tears from his eyes. "I'm sorry, Sam. I didn't mean to be such a baby. I don't know the last time I acted like this. Probably when my dad passed away."

I put a mock scowl on my face and shook my finger at him. "Now listen here, Hank Johnson. You are the bravest, kindest, sincerest, handsomest man I know. I should have bitten my tongue before implicating Aaron in Edgar's death."

Hank placed one of his strong, well-shaped fingers to my lips. "Hush. You can say anything you like to me. Always remember that. I thought I had made progress with Aaron. He has a good job, is thinking about going to culinary school, and Joy is a fabulous girlfriend. Then he goes off, gets drunk and, to top it off, causes a scene at the Taste of Wings Falls. And now he's a major suspect in the murder of Edgar Jensen."

I brushed back the wayward curl and caressed his cheek. The after-five stubble sent tingles up my arm. "Hank, you are the best big brother ever. Don't ever doubt it. You've done everything you can for Aaron, and I'm sure he appreciates it. Think about it… Where would he be now without you taking him in? Probably roaming the streets of Albany with some gang. Wait a minute. Did you say Edgar Jensen was murdered? Is it definite?"

Hank nodded. "Yeah, forensic figured there was no way, even if it was wobbly, the pumpkin could have fallen off of Scooter Dickenson's truck by itself. Someone had to have given it help."

I nodded. Those were my thoughts, too. "Hank, I know your brother didn't kill Edgar. He may have been angry with him, but he wouldn't act so foolishly as to risk everything he's been working for since he moved in with you." I reached over to the coffee table and handed him his beer. "Here, before this gets warm, enjoy." Then I lifted my glass of Riesling to my lips. Its sweet taste danced on my tongue.

"I pray you're right, Sam, but youth often acts first then thinks later." Hank raised his beer to his lips and took a large swallow.

I swirled the wine in my glass. "Yes, but there are other people who had a reason to see Edgar dead—Franny Goodway, Bill Collins, Joe Peters, and the most likely suspect—his wife, Carol. They all had more of a reason to want Edgar dead than Aaron."

Hank raised an eyebrow and grinned. "Are the sleuth cousins at it again?"

I blushed. Hank was well aware of Candie's and my penchant for getting involved in murder investigations. I think he had given up on trying to warn me off of, as he liked to say, "sticking my pretty little nose where it doesn't belong." His words, not mine.

Hank placed his beer bottle on the coffee table and pulled me to him. He rested his chin on my head. "Let's hear your theories on who might have set Scooter's pumpkin in motion."

I snuggled up to his warm body and nestled into the folds of his sports jacket. I held up one hand and flicked up a finger. "First, there is Joe Peters. His wife Portia is having a mid-life crisis and needs a purpose for her life now that both kids have gone off to college. I told you Candie and I ran into her at Discount World, and she didn't have one kind word for Edgar. Either Joe or Portia could have done him in." I flipped up a second finger. "Then there is Bill Collins. Candie said Mark got an earful at City Hall from Bill about Edgar and his shady banking techniques. Or maybe even his sons, Chris or David. They stand to lose their family heritage if they don't get a loan to make the improvements needed to their restaurant. Think about it. Their grandfather started The Round Up. That's a lot to lose if they have to close the restaurant. Third…" Up went another digit. "I hate to put Franny Goodway on the list. I know she needs money to help Joy with her college expenses, but I just can't see her harming a flea, let alone murdering Edgar." My pinky finger joined the others standing at attention. "Finally, there's the one person who is always the prime suspect—the wife, Carol. I haven't quite pinned her reason down yet. But why would a supposedly grieving wife be at Discount World the day after her husband's death? I'm not going to put Aaron on the list because I know he didn't do it." Although secretly, I worried about Aaron. After all, he did publicly threaten Edgar. Would that be enough to make him a suspect—even the *main* suspect—in the eyes of the police?

Hank hugged me to him. "Thank you for your faith in my baby brother."

"He reminds me of his big brother, so I know it isn't in him to do such a thing. Get drunk maybe, or defend the woman he loves, definitely, but kill—no."

Hank chuckled. "You know me too well." He tugged on one of my curls. "I'd defend this woman I love to my death."

"I love you, too." I reached up and pulled his head down so I could kiss his inviting lips.

When we came up for air, Hank frowned. "Wait a minute. You didn't mention Clint Higgins. He has as much reason to want Edgar dead as Franny and Bill. He was also seeking a loan from the bank."

I shook my head. "Not anymore."

Hank sat up straighter so he could face me. "What? Why?"

"At Loopy Ladies this morning, Marybeth and I got into a conversation about Clint attempting to get a loan from Edgar."

Hank smiled. "I can imagine how it came about."

I poked him in the ribs. "Do you want to hear my reason for leaving him off my suspect list or not?"

"Okay, spill it."

"Marybeth said Clint wasn't about to put up with Edgar's demand for a 'special fee' and went to Sandy Hill Savings and Loan and obtained the money he needed for his new appliances from them."

Hank ran a hand over his stubbled chin. "I wonder why the others didn't do that."

I shrugged my shoulders. "Your guess is as good as mine. People get attached to their hometown banks. The tellers know you and your family. They are our friends and neighbors."

Porkchop jumped up on the sofa and nudged his small head onto Hank's lap. Hank reached down and patted him. "Have we been neglecting you, boy? That's one of the nice things about living in a small town. Coming from a big city like Albany, we weren't familiar with our bank people. Most times, you went into the bank, did your business, then left. There was no chit-chat about your family or how you were doing, like here in Wings Falls."

I stifled a yawn with my hand. "I'm sorry. Believe me, it's not the company." I plucked at my sweatshirt. "As you can see, I've been cleaning most of the day."

Hank pulled me back into his embrace and kissed me. "You look beautiful no matter what you wear, but I know you must be tired, so I'll head on home. I think Aaron's out with Joy tonight. I better see to Nina."

"You should have brought Nina with you. The both of you could have stayed over," I said, thinking of how the night could have ended.

"I didn't know if I'd be welcome, and I thought it might be better to leave her home," Hank said.

I traced circles on Hank's chest with my finger. "All is forgotten. I love the roses. They are beautiful."

"Beautiful flowers for a beautiful lady." Hank lifted my hand off his chest and placed a lingering kiss on my palm.

He pushed himself off the sofa. Porkchop jumped down and followed Hank and me to the door. Once there, Hank pulled me to him. He tapped the end of my nose. "Remember, I love you and don't want you getting hurt by sticking that pretty nose where it shouldn't be."

Porkchop yipped. Hank scratched between his ears. "Take care of her, good buddy, when I'm not here. You know she tends to get herself in trouble when I'm not around."

Porkchop yipped again as if to say, *You can count on me.*

Little did Porkchop know what a tall order it would be.

CHAPTER TWENTY-EIGHT

———

I waited at the open front door until Hank's taillights faded into the dark of night. "Come on, Porkchop. It's time for us to hit the sack." I walked back into the living room and grabbed Hank's empty beer bottle from the coffee table. A small amount of wine remained in the bottom of my glass. I tipped my head back and finished off the wine. Porkchop followed me into the kitchen.

A smile spread across my face as I glanced at the beautiful roses sitting on the counter. "We need to find a better place for these gorgeous blooms." Porkchop cocked his head as I pondered the best place to display them. I picked up the vase then walked over to the kitchen table and set it in the center. "How about here, Porkchop? I can enjoy them every morning as I drink my morning cup of decaf and eat a sesame seed bagel." Yep, this would be the perfect place. What better way to start my day?

"You know, Porkie, in twenty-five years of marriage, George never brought me any flowers, not even dandelions. Guess it said a lot about him." A growl rumbled up from his throat. "Yeah, I know. He wasn't your favorite person. I should have paid attention when you growled whenever he came near me. I would have been a lot smarter. Oh well. Luckily he's not our problem anymore. Anna has to deal with him now."

Porkchop strutted over to his water bowl and slurped it dry.

"Come on. After drinking all that water, I'm sure you have to go do your business before we go to bed." I patted my leg for him to follow me to the back door and opened it. He trotted down the steps to the fenced-in backyard. I stood watching him and noticed a car I didn't recognize driving slowly past my house. I rubbed my hands up and down the sleeves of my sweatshirt. A chill ran through me, and it wasn't from the cool night air. Was this person checking me out? Maybe I was being paranoid, but now I was sorry I hadn't insisted on Hank spending the night.

Porkchop had finished his nightly routine. "Come on, Porkie. Let's turn in."

I craned my neck to see where the strange car had gone, but it must have turned off the street, as I no longer saw its taillights. Porkchop hopped back up the steps. Once he was inside, I locked the door, turned off the kitchen lights, then made sure the living room door was locked and latched.

With the doors locked, windows checked, pajamas donned, face washed, teeth brushed, alarm set, I finally climbed into bed and pulled the covers up to my chin. Porkchop lay curled up at the end of my bed. I patted my pillow. "Porkchop, come here and snuggle with me."

He raised his head and gave me a questioning look. His usual place to sleep was at my feet, but tonight I needed the warmth of his long furry body to calm the nerves I felt after seeing the strange car cruise past my house. I had the eerie feeling that whoever was behind the wheel was staring right at me as either he or she, I wasn't able to tell in the dark, drove by.

Porkchop waddled over the disheveled blankets and nestled in the crook of my arm. I pulled him closer so my face rested against his warm body. "Porkie, do you think the driver of the car is Edgar's murderer?"

Unfortunately, he was unable to answer my question. Before long, I heard his soft snores. Hopefully, I'd soon join him in a peaceful, dream-free sleep.

* * *

An annoying buzzing jarred me awake. Without opening my eyes, I reached over to my nightstand to silence it. I squinted at the neon green numbers on my alarm clock. Seven o'clock.

"Rise and shine, Porkchop. I need to check in with Bob Spellman to make sure the issue with our book is settled and then work on promoting it. If you're going to be a big star, I have to make sure you get all the attention I can muster." Porkchop stirred beside me. He stretched his long body, turned his head towards me, and gave me a doggie kiss on my cheek.

I hugged his lean body to me then flipped back the covers and swung my legs out of bed. He dug his head farther under the covers. "Aw, Porkie, I love you, too, but we have to get a move on." I scooped him up and placed him on my cold bedroom floor.

"Eww, eww," I said, dancing over to my fuzzy slippers.

Porkchop followed me out of my bedroom to the kitchen. While he was outside doing his business, I plugged in my coffeepot, placed a bagel in the toaster, filled his water bowl, and dumped kibble into his dog-shaped food bowl.

After he finished his outside duty, we both settled down to eat our meal. As I ate, I enjoyed the beautiful bouquet sitting in the middle of the table. My heart ached for Hank as I remembered how upset he was thinking Aaron might be a murderer. When this was all over, I was going to have a talk with Aaron and, hopefully, make him understand how much his big brother loved him. I chuckled out loud. "Porkchop, I'm starting to sound like Memaw Parker, imparting my wisdom to the young. If that doesn't work, I could always march him to the woodshed and let a hickory stick do the talking."

Porkchop whined in response.

"Porkie, I'm just kidding, about the hickory stick, that is, but I will let him know how upset Hank was."

Porkchop thumped his tail on the kitchen floor. I think this was his sign of approval that I had revised my plan of action.

* * *

"Porkchop, I can't take any more staring at this computer." I rubbed by eyes then leaned back in my chair and stretched my arms over my head. I glanced at my Timex watch, a present from my parents many years ago. Three hours had passed since I had set my butt into my desk chair. I had accomplished a lot in that time, and not once did I go on Facebook, not that I wasn't tempted.

"I need a new bottle of shampoo, and I'm out of my daily vitamins. How does a trip to Eagle Drug Store sound to you?"

Porkchop slipped his long body out of the dog bed I had placed at my feet in my den/office and stretched. With his rear end in the air, he yawned and turned his head towards me.

I reached down and scratched his back. "If you think you need more beauty sleep, you can always stay home."

He thumped his tail on the carpet.

"I guess you're awake now, and we both need to see some civilization. Holed up inside all morning isn't good for my brain."

* * *

Fifteen minutes later, after I'd brushed my teeth, combed my hair, and fed Porkchop some of his kibble, we were seated in my Bug and on our way to Eagle Drug Store for the shampoo and vitamins I needed.

"Porkchop, pups aren't really welcome in the store. You'll have to wait for me here. I won't be long."

I lowered the window so he'd have plenty of fresh air and placed a rawhide bone on the seat next to him. It would keep him busy while I purchased the few items I needed. I patted his head then opened the car door. A crisp breeze stirred my curly hair. I pulled my navy quilted vest closer to my body and scurried into the warmth of the drugstore.

As I stood in the shampoo aisle searching for my favorite brand, a hand reached in front of me and grabbed a bottle off of the shelf. "Hi, Sam. The Taste of Wings Falls certainly had some excitement this weekend."

I turned to see Shirley Carrigan beside me. She was dressed in what looked like workout pants and shirt. They both clung to her muscled legs and torso. "Hi. Did you just come from the gym?"

Shirley nodded her head. "Yeah, I ran out of my favorite shampoo and thought I'd run in before I head over to the pet shelter."

In her youth, Shirley had been a rising star in the Women's Wrestling Federation, going by the name of Shirley the Slammer. Now she owned a pet shelter, providing a safe home for abandoned animals.

A woman's high-pitched giggle caught both of our attentions. I stood on my tiptoes to glance over the shelves, and my mouth dropped open.

CHAPTER TWENTY-NINE

———

I shook my head and pointed to the woman two aisles over from Shirley and me. "Do you see what she's doing? I can't believe my eyes. She's flirting with the store manager, and her husband isn't even in the ground."

Shirley frowned. A look of disgust crossed her face. "It doesn't surprise me. I've seen her cozying up to guys at the gym."

"Really?" I asked. I felt as upset as Shirley did about Carol Jensen's behavior, especially after the way my own marriage had ended with my ex cheating on me.

"Yeah, she's known as the 'red hot momma' around the gym. She loves to show off to the guys with her aptitude for lifting weights. She'll even challenge them to weight-lifting contests."

"But she's so tiny. How could she do that?" I puzzled this over in my brain. If she was so adept at lifting weights, was she strong enough to push a big pumpkin onto her late husband? Like Candie had said, the spouse was usually the main suspect in a murder. She did appear to be upset with Edgar on Saturday. How many wives would tolerate their husband openly making a pass at another woman like he did with Joy? Was she mad enough to kill him?

"She comes to the gym at least five days a week. Sometimes more." Shirley leaned closer to me. "It's rumored she's having an affair with Lonnie, the gym's trainer."

I blinked. This was getting curiouser and curiouser as Alice said in *Wonderland*. "But she's married." Duh, so was my ex, but that didn't stop him from playing the horizontal tango with our funeral parlor's secretary. Did she want to get rid of Edgar so she could hook up with Lonnie? Then again, she was already cozy with the trainer when Edgar was alive. Did she want to ditch Edgar and he wouldn't let her go?

"I even saw them at the Racino a couple of weeks ago. They looked pretty cozy playing the slot machines together."

This was a lot to absorb standing in the shampoo aisle. "Did you say anything to them?"

"Nope. It's none of my business what people do with their lives. I have enough to contend with. I'll stick with the animals in my shelter. They don't ask for anything but to keep their bellies full, a place to sleep, and love."

"I'll agree with you there. Speaking of animals, I'd better finish up with what I came in here for and get back to my car. His lordship, Porkchop, awaits me there."

Shirley laughed. "He certainly looked cute in his cowboy hat on Saturday. He would have gotten my vote as winner of the pet costume parade if I were allowed to vote."

I gave Shirley a side hug. "Ahhh, thank you. That's kind of you to say."

As Shirley walked away, I looked both ways to see if the coast was clear then dug into my red Michael Kors bag for my phone. I stood on my tiptoes and snapped a picture of Carol reaching up and planting a kiss on the store manager's cheek. When I showed the compromising picture to Hank, I thought it would go a long way to prove Aaron and my friends not guilty of Edgar's murder.

I quickly snagged a bottle of vitamins and checked out through the self-checkout kiosk. I exited the store and walked over to my car. Porkchop stood with his paws on the driver's-side window barking. I carefully eased the side door of my Bug open so Porkchop wouldn't tumble out and tossed my purchases in the back seat. "Were you a good boy while I was gone? I'm sorry I took so long, but I ran into Shirley Carrigan, and she gave me an earful about Carol Jensen." Porkchop whined and put his paws on my lap. "Sweetie, you know you have to sit in your seat while I drive." I picked up his paws and placed them on the passenger seat. When I pulled my hands away from his paws, red stained my fingers. I stared at them then pulled him back onto my lap, afraid he had cut himself on something I had carelessly left in the car. I hugged him to me as I checked his paws but didn't find any wounds.

"Porkchop, what's this? Are your paws bleeding? What happened when I was in the store? Did you cut yourself?" I didn't know how that could have happened. I scanned my car but didn't find any sharp objects or surfaces. Whose blood could this be? A shiny object on his seat caught my eye—a pearl button. How could it have gotten here? I looked down at the vest I wore. A zipper ran up its front. No buttons. Same with the long-sleeved T-shirt I wore underneath—no buttons. I shook my head in confusion. I reached into my handbag and pulled out a packet of tissues and cleaned his paws. There were no wounds that I could detect, and he didn't flinch when I touched them. He reached up and licked my face. I took it as a good sign that all was well with him. I was still puzzled at the red that had stained his paws. Maybe it wasn't blood. I had bought some strawberries the other day at the Shop and Save. Maybe a few had tumbled out of my shopping bag and I didn't notice them, but Porkchop's keen nose had discovered the berries while I was in the drugstore.

"Porkchop, you wouldn't believe who I saw inside the store." Porkchop cocked his head to listen to me. He was the best listener. He always gave me his full attention and never contradicted what I said. Such a good pup. I patted his head then started my car and shifted into reverse. "I have a picture I want to show Hank. I believe it will prove that someone had a bigger motive to kill Edgar Jensen than Aaron and Franny. I still don't know about Bill Collins and his sons or Sandy and Portia Peters." I gave Porkchop a side-eye as I headed the Bug towards the Wings Falls Police station. His chocolate-brown eyes stared up at me. I had his full attention. "You see, I saw Carol Jensen smooching with the store manager."

Porkchop yipped.

"Yep. It's what I think, too. If she was so in love with her husband, why would she be making a pass at another man and so soon after his death? Mighty strange, don't you think?"

It was only a ten-minute drive to the police station. I pulled my car into a slot next to a black and white. "Come on, Porkie, let's go pay Hank a visit and show him the picture I took of the widow Carol."

Porkchop's slim body shook with excitement at the mention of Hank's name. He leapt into my arms when I opened the passenger-side door. I placed him on the ground and reached in for my purse. He tugged on his leash as we approached the one-story. red brick police building.

"You have to behave yourself in here, Porkchop." He strained at his leash.

I pulled open the heavy metal door of the station and walked into a large reception area. I walked over to the counter, where Wanda Thurston sat behind bulletproof glass. A headset was nestled in her black curls. She looked up at Porkchop and me and smiled.

"Hi Sam, and welcome, Porkchop. It's great seeing you. Are you here to see Hank?" Wanda was the PCO—or public communications officer—for the station. No one got past her without her permission.

I nodded. "Yes, if you could please let him know."

A smile spread across Wanda's face, her white teeth a sharp contrast to her dark skin. "Sure. Have a seat, and I'll let him know you two are here."

I settled into one of the metal chairs that lined the room. Porkchop sat at my feet on the tiled floor. Across from me, a photo of New York's governor stared down at me. A buzzer sounded, and my eyes snapped to the door that separated the reception area from the main workings of the station.

Hank strode through the door. "To what do I owe this surprise? Not that I mind. You have certainly brought some much-needed sunshine into my day."

Porkchop broke from my grasp and raced over to Hank. His leash trailed along after him, bouncing on the hard floor.

I rose from my chair. "Porkchop, come back here."

I heard a chuckle come from Wanda.

Hank reached down and petted his admirer. "It's okay."

"I have some information I think you might find interesting. Can we go back to your office?"

Hank nodded towards Wanda, and she released the lock on the door Hank had just come through. I was always amazed at the buzz of activity that greeted a person when they entered the inner workings of the station. Officers sat at metal desks typing away on laptops, talking on phones, or conversing with each other. I had gotten to know some of these policemen in the year since I'd started dating Hank, and a number of them called "Hello" to me or nodded in our direction. Noticeably absent was Joe Peters. He usually had a snarky comment or two for me when I passed through this room. Sometimes, I was quick-witted enough to sling one back at him. I would smile and let them roll off my back. After all, these exchanges had been going on since we were in kindergarten.

Hank opened the door to his office and motioned for Porkchop and me to enter. Once again, I sat in one of those state-issued uncomfortable chairs. Porkchop sat at my feet.

Hank leaned against his metal desk. "What brings you and my buddy here? Not that I mind."

I smiled at his tie choice for today, Popeye, then dug into my purse and pulled out my phone. I flipped it open and searched for the picture I had taken of Carol and her current squeeze.

CHAPTER THIRTY

I handed the phone to Hank. My fingers tingled as his brushed against mine.

His eyebrow rose. "Interesting. It only proves Edgar's wife isn't exactly mourning his passing."

My mouth dropped open. "What do you mean it only proves Carol isn't a grieving widow? Don't you see? She should be at the top of your suspect list in his death. She certainly is on mine."

Hank looked at me and frowned. Oops. I did a mental palm plant on my forehead. I should have left off my last statement.

"Don't you see? She's been fooling around on her husband. She and Shirley Carrigan go to the same gym, and Shirley told me she is having an affair with a trainer named Lonnie at the gym. Shirley also mentioned Carol does a lot of weight training there and would be strong enough to shove the pumpkin on Edgar. This exonerates Aaron."

Hank slowly shook his head. "I wish everything you told me pointed Edgar's murder to Carol, but she has an alibi."

I couldn't believe what Hank was telling me. "No. No way."

Hank took my hand in his and brushed back a strand of hair that had fallen over my face. I know you are trying your hardest to exonerate my brother and your friends. Believe me, I am, too. But we questioned this Lonnie, and he said Carol was at the gym at the time of Edgar's death."

I sat up straight in my chair. "He's lying to protect his bimbo."

Hank stroked the back of my hand and shook his head. "There is a security camera at the gym. It backs him up. Also, other people were working out at the same time, too. We questioned them, and they can vouch for her being there."

My spirits sank right down to my sneakers. I was sure Carol had killed her husband. All the evidence pointed right to her—she was seen arguing with her husband at the Taste of Wings Falls, Shirley said from Carol's workouts at the gym that she was strong enough to have pushed the pumpkin onto Edgar, flattening him like a pancake, and for me the biggest clue—she was cheating on her husband.

Oh! Oh! Another idea floated around my brain. Why was Edgar charging people an extra fee for their loans from the bank? Was Carol behind the reason for these "special fees"? Why did she and Edgar need this money? Could Carol have paid someone to bump off Edgar? She had the perfect alibi—working out at the gym, where she would be seen by others at the time of good ol' hubby's death. Caught on camera no less, so no one could question her whereabouts. But with Edgar dead, there would go the extra money from the "special fees."

"What are you thinking about? I can tell you have something running around that cute head of yours."

I snapped back to the present at Hank's question. "Um, nothing. I was thinking about what you told me. I guess you're right. Carol can be eliminated as a suspect."

Hank pulled me out of my chair and into his arms. "Why do I get the impression you aren't completely convinced of our findings?"

I blushed. Hank could read me so well.

"Sam, our guys are good and thorough. They know what they are doing. Please, leave this to the professionals. I don't want anything to happen to you." He kissed me.

I leaned back and looked into his crystal-blue eyes. Eyes that made my knees go weak when they turned smokey with desire. "I'm sorry. I know your guys are the best, but I can't let go of Carol being a possible suspect."

"I won't tell you what to do or not to do. I learned that's impossible, but promise me you'll be careful." He pulled me against his muscled chest and kissed the top of my head.

I could hear his heart beating under Popeye. I silently prayed that, like Popeye, Hank would be "strong to the finish" and be able to prove his brother and our friends innocent of Edgar's murder.

"Are you going to have spinach for dinner?" I asked.

Hank stepped back from me and frowned. "Huh?"

I pointed to his tie. "You know, Popeye's favorite veggie—spinach."

Hank laughed. "Nah. Until this case is solved, I'll probably be eating a ton of take out."

These murder cases sure cut into our alone time. I was being selfish, but my heart ached and I missed him, as did his buddy, Porkchop.

Hank placed a finger under my chin and lifted my face. "Why the sad look? You know the downside of being a cop. Are you sure you can handle being involved with me? This isn't a nine-to-five job."

I hugged him tighter to me. A tear slid down my cheek. "Don't ever think that. I know your life isn't always your own, but I can't imagine what it would be like if you weren't a part of my life— or Porkchop's," I added, looking down at Porkchop, who snoozed next to the chair I'd vacated.

Hank chuckled. "Good, then you two are stuck with Nina and me." He touched the gold heart hanging around my neck. "Remember what I had engraved on the back of this heart— MTYLTT." He flipped the heart over and tapped it with his finger.

The message was engraved not only on the back of the gold heart but also on my own heart. "More Than Yesterday, Less Than Tomorrow," I said.

Hank caressed my face. "I love you more than yesterday, but less than tomorrow," he breathed against my lips before he lowered his to mine.

A knock at the door caused us to jump apart. Porkchop awoke and started to bark.

"Come in," Hank called out. He ran an unsteady hand through his wavy hair.

Officer Reed poked his head in the door. "Sir, the test results for the barbeque served at the Taste are back." I had met Officer Reed in the summer when an ex-fiancé of Candie's was found murdered in her home. He was relatively new on the force, out of the police academy for less than a year.

"Come on in, Reed. Sam was leaving." Hank circled his desk and sat down.

I gathered up Porkchop's leash and my purse. "Bye, Hank. We'll talk later?"

"I'll give you a call this evening. I can't say what time. It will probably be a late night. We'll see what we can do about going out to eat somewhere."

I said hello to Officer Reed on my way out of Hank's office. He returned my greeting with: "Good afternoon, ma'am." Geez, a ma'am? This young recruit made me feel all of my fifty-five years.

As I closed the door, I overheard him say to Hank the words lavender and Franny Goodway's name.

Nooooo, I screamed in my head. Franny wouldn't have placed an ingredient in her barbeque that could have made people sick. I didn't believe it. I had hoped that I was wrong about the lavender, but that didn't mean Franny, Joy, or Aaron had placed it there. I knew they wouldn't do something that would endanger the health of their customers.

* * *

I sat in my Bug in the station's parking lot, pondering what I had learned in Hank's office. "Porkchop, I don't believe it." I smacked the steering wheel with the palm of my hand. "No, I won't believe it. Franny would never do such a thing, and for what reason? What would making people sick on her barbeque get her?"

Porkchop sat on the passenger seat listening intently to my rant.

"I'm going to drop you off at home and give your aunt Candie a call." I glanced up at the Bug's digital clock. It read four o'clock. "She should be finished at work by now. I'll see if she's free to go to Sweetie Pie's for a cup of coffee." What I hoped to accomplish by going there, I had no idea, but I needed to talk to Franny and see if she remembered anything more about who bought her pulled pork. Maybe someone was a little too close to the chafing dishes and could have slipped the lavender in. But first I should call Montana Casey and ask if she recalls who she sold lavender to on Saturday. I knew it was a long shot, but I had to do something.

I dug into my purse for my phone and scrolled down to my saved numbers. Montana's was one of them. She answered on the second ring. "Hi Montana. I was wondering if you happened to recall any of the people you sold lavender to on Saturday at the fair. I know you were swamped, but was there anyone who stood out in your mind? Carol Jensen? Aaron?"

"I was so busy," Montana said, "but now that you mention it, yes. Aaron bought my lavender oil."

My heart sank. Tears welled up in my eyes. "Aaron?" I repeated Montana's answer with disbelief. Why would he have bought lavender? I thanked Montana for the information. Now I wondered if my call was such a good idea.

CHAPTER THIRTY-ONE

————

I pulled into my driveway and rested my forehead on my steering wheel. I heaved a deep sigh. "Porkchop, what are we going to do to prove my friends aren't guilty of murder? I was positive Carol Jensen did Edgar in."

Porkchop scooched onto my lap and licked my hand. I cradled his small head in my hands and stroked his soft fur. "Porkchop, you are the best, you know. Just the best."

He backed up onto the passenger seat and barked as if to say, *Yep, and don't you forget it. Now let's go inside and fill my kibble bowl.*

"Okay, I hear you. Your tummy is calling." I grabbed my purse from the back seat then reached for his leash. As I exited the Bug, my feet crunched on the leaves covering my driveway.

I made a mental note to call Lawns R Us, the guys I used to mow my lawn in the summer, shovel snow in the winter, and rake my leaves in the fall. I glanced at my home, a brick one-story, as Porkchop and I walked up the walkway to my front door. I was raised here. My parents signed it over to me when they retired to Florida over five years ago.

As I walked in the front door, my phone rang. I dropped Porkchop's leash then reached into my purse for my phone. The caller ID showed me Candie's name. "Hi cuz, I was going to call you."

"You were? Good. I'm lonely. Do you want to go out for a bite to eat?" Candie's voice held a slight whine to it. I could imagine her sitting on the tufted velvet couch in her living room with a pout on her face.

I laughed. "What, no Mark to keep you company?"

"No, he has a Chamber of Commerce meeting tonight. It's only Cuddles, Dixie, and me sitting here all alone on the sofa."

I smiled to myself. I was right. I knew my cousin so well. "I was planning on going over to Sweetie Pie's. I want to talk to Franny about the barbeque she served on Saturday. I also need to have a chat with Aaron. Do you want to come?"

"Aaron? How come? You can't think he had anything to do with the barbeque, do you?"

I told Candie about my phone call to Montana.

"Oh, oh. Are we going to do some sleuthing?" The sound of Candie clapping her hands with excitement rang in my ears.

"Yes, we're going to do some sleuthing. I'll be by in about fifteen minutes. I have to feed Porkchop and let him out, and then I'll head over."

"I'll be waiting for you on my porch," Candie replied then hung up.

I shoved my phone back into my purse then glanced down at Porkchop. "Come on, sweetheart. Momma will fill your kibble bowl and let you out, and then I've got to get over to your aunt Candie's so the Sleuth Cousins can ride again."

* * *

Candie jumped off the wicker swing hanging in the corner of her porch and bounded down the steps towards the Bug before I even came to a stop. She flung open the passenger side door and slid in. She turned to me, excitement flushing her cheeks. "Okay, what are we going to investigate at Sweetie Pie's?"

I placed the car in reverse and looked over my shoulder as I backed out of her driveway. "I stopped in the police station earlier today to talk to Hank about Carol Jensen."

"What about Carol Jensen? You haven't told me anything about her."

Uh-oh. True, Candie was usually the first person I spoke to about all things important, but things happened so fast today, I hadn't had the time. I gave Candie a side-glance as I drove towards Sweetie Pie's. "I needed to go to Eagle Drug Store this morning to buy a few things, and while I was there, I ran into Shirley Carrigan."

Candie waggled her jeweled fingers at me. I wasn't telling my story fast enough for her. "Annnd?" she drawled.

I returned my attention to the road. "And she told me about Carol Jensen having an affair with the trainer at the gym they go to."

"Doesn't surprise me," Candie said.

We were stopped at a red light. "What?" I asked, glancing at her.

"She looks the type."

The light turned green, and I returned my eyes to the road in front of me. "What's 'the type'?"

"You know, hanging all over the men. I can usually spot a cheater when I see one," Candie said.

"Your 'cheater radar' must have been broken when it came to George," I said, referring to my cheating ex-husband.

Candie cleared her throat. "Yeah, but you know I never did like him. That has to count for something. But tell me more about your talk with Shirley. Also, why didn't you call and tell me about this?" She managed to insert a hurt tone into her voice.

I smiled. An Oscar-winning actress had nothing on my cousin. "She also said Carol worked out regularly at the gym and thought, from watching Carol lift weights, she could be strong enough to push the pumpkin onto Edgar."

"Hmmm, interesting," Candie said.

"That's not the most interesting thing, though," I said, turning into Sweetie Pie's nearly empty parking lot.

"Don't keep me in suspense. It's bad enough you didn't call me to tell me all about this," Candie said.

I shifted the car into park then turned to her. "You were at work, and I didn't want to disturb you. Plus, I wanted to get to the police station to show Hank what I discovered."

"Since when don't you call me at work? What did you want to show Hank?"

I reached into the back seat and pulled my Michael Kors purse towards me. I dug out my phone and flipped it open. "Look what I snapped while I was standing in the shampoo aisle." I turned the phone towards Candie.

Candie's Passion Pink lips formed an *O* as she reached for my phone. "What did Hank say about Carol and this picture?"

I frowned. I hated to even say the words. "Carol has an alibi for the time of Edgar's murder."

Candie sat staring at the picture. "Drat, and she was the perfect suspect."

She handed me back my phone, and I tucked it into my purse. "I know, but I'm not ruling her out yet. I feel it in my bones she was up to something on Saturday, but I haven't figured it out."

"We will. Never fear, we will." Candie opened her door. A cool breeze stirred the auburn curls skimming her shoulders.

When Candie joined me on my side of the car, I pointed towards the practically empty parking lot. "I've never seen so few cars. Sweetie Pie's has been a hit since the day Franny opened its doors over fifteen years ago. I hope Franny isn't sick or anything."

I pushed open the door to Sweetie Pie's and glanced around the room. Only two of the five stools in front of the counter facing the kitchen were occupied. I nodded to Al Gorman and Clyde Holden, the town's most popular barber, as they swiveled on their stools when Candie and I walked in.

Franny emerged from the kitchen. Her face looked drawn. The usual sparkle was gone from her brown eyes.

CHAPTER THIRTY-TWO

———

Franny nodded at us. "Hi, Sam, Candie."

"Evening," Candie and I said in unison.

"You can sit anywhere you want. As you can see, you've got the pick of the booths this evening." Franny gave a halfhearted chuckle. She swept the room with her thin hand.

My eyes followed her hand. I'd never seen Sweetie Pie's so empty. The red vinyl–clad booths hugging three of the glossy white walls all stood empty. A lump formed in my throat, and I swallowed hard to keep tears from flooding my eyes.

"How about our usual booth by the window?" I asked, pointing to our favorite booth Candie and I claimed every Sunday.

Franny snatched two menus off a service station and followed us to the booth. Candie and I slid into the seats. Franny placed the menus in front of us. "You ladies want me to fetch you a cup of coffee while you look at the menus? Aaron's cooked up a great beef stew this evening. Right, Aaron?" A window into the kitchen was situated behind the counter in the front of Sweetie Pie's.

At the mention of his name, Aaron looked up and waved to us.

"Oh, my. What happened to his hand?" It was heavily bandaged under the clear plastic glove he wore.

Franny frowned. "He said he was experimenting with a new recipe at home this morning and burned it. One of the dangers of being a cook."

I nodded and handed my menu back to Franny. "I guess you're right. I don't have to take a look at this. The beef stew sounds great, especially on a fall day like this."

"I'll have the same," Candie said, handing Franny her menu.

"By the way, where's Joy? I didn't notice her when we walked in," I said.

Franny frowned. "She's home."

"Oh, no. She hasn't come down with something, has she? The flu bug runs rampant in the fall," Candie said, frowning.

Franny shook her head. Her curly ponytail swishing about her shoulders. "No, she's been suffering from a migraine off and on since Saturday night."

I'd had a few doozy headaches, especially when I was going through my divorce from George. "I hope she's feeling better soon. Give her my best."

Franny slid a pad of paper out of her apron pocket and jotted down our order. "I will. This barbeque nonsense has all of us worried. Look around the café. It's practically empty. No one wants to eat here. They probably think I'm going to poison them." Franny's thin shoulders slumped as she turned and walked back to the kitchen to give Aaron our ticket.

I leaned over the worn red Formica tabletop and whispered to Candie, "I can't believe people would think Franny would purposely add something to her food to poison her customers."

"It's one of the drawbacks of living in a small town—gossip. Before the police even had the official report of the tainted barbeque being Franny's, folks pointed the finger at her. By now they might even believe she's some mass murderer and put arsenic in her food," Candie said.

I shook my head to dispel that thought. "Not our Franny. How could anyone think such a thing?"

I loved my hometown and wouldn't want to live anywhere else, but I had to agree with my cousin. People liked to dish the dirt on others, and the juicier the better.

Since the kitchen wasn't busy, Franny returned within minutes with steaming hot bowls of beef stew and mugs of coffee. Slices of fresh-baked bread sat on a plate next to them. The aromas of both had my mouth watering. "Enjoy, ladies, but save room for a slice of my banana cream pie."

I laughed. "Franny, I'm going to waddle out of here after I eat all of this." I pointed to the stew and bread she'd placed before me.

"It makes my heart sing to see folks enjoying Sweetie Pie's food," Franny said then turned towards the kitchen.

"We definitely will," Candie said, picking up her fork.

* * *

I swiped my mouth with a paper napkin and groaned. "I don't know when I've ever tasted a better beef stew. Aaron certainly has a magic touch in the kitchen."

Candie, ever the Southern lady, dabbed at the corners of her mouth with her napkin. "I have to agree with you. It was a very tasty stew. He has a lot of talent in the kitchen."

"Yeah, Hank and I are hoping he goes to Wing Falls Community College and enrolls in their culinary arts program."

"It would be a fantastic career for him, especially since he lives in a tourist area where there are a ton of restaurants."

I placed my napkin on the table and started to rise from the booth's seat.

Candie raised an eyebrow in question. "You going to the ladies' room?

I shook my head. "No. Since the restaurant isn't busy, I thought I'd go question Aaron about his lavender purchase."

Candie squeezed my hand as I stood. "Good luck. I know this isn't easy for you."

A weak smile formed on my lips. "Thanks. I'll need it."

I walked over to the open window into the kitchen. "Aaron, can I speak to you for a moment?"

He put down the spoon he'd been using to stir whatever he was cooking in a pot on the large stove. "Sure. Give me a moment to turn off the burner."

It always amazed me how much he looked like Hank, with the same blue eyes and dark brown curly hair.

He wiped his uninjured hand on his apron and walked over to the window. "What can I do for you, Sam?"

"Weell, ummm…" I couldn't get my question out.

Concern crossed Aaron's face. "What is it, Sam? Is something the matter?"

"Aaron, I hate to ask this, but I was talking to Montana Casey, and she said you bought a vial of lavender from her on Saturday at the fair."

"Yeah, I did. Joy loves the scent of lavender, and after the way that jerk Jensen made a pass at her, she was really upset. I thought I'd do something nice for her and buy her some. Why do you ask?" He frowned. "Wait. Is this about Franny's barbeque? You think I put something in it. How could you, Sam? I thought you knew me better than that."

Great. Now I felt about two inches tall. "I'm sorry, Aaron, but I had to ask."

"Yeah. Well, you asked, and now I've got to get back to work." He turned and walked back to the stove. He shoved the spoon he'd been using into the pot and stirred with angry movements.

With heavy steps and my shoulders slumped, I returned to my seat.

"Didn't go well?" Candie asked.

I shook my head. "That's putting it mildly. A disaster would be more like it. It'll be a long time before we're back on friendly terms."

"So, what do you think? Did he mess with Franny's barbeque?"

"No, he said he bought the lavender as a present for Joy. I believe he's innocent, and not just because he's Hank's brother. He's too in love with Joy to jeopardize their relationship by doing something that stupid."

"Ladies, are you ready for a piece of my fabulous banana cream pie? It will be on the house. As you can see from my lack of customers, I haven't had very many takers. I don't want it to go to waste." Franny nodded to the deserted room. Except for Candie and me, we were the only people remaining. Al and Clyde were gone.

I welcomed Franny's diversion from my troubling thoughts and patted the seat next to me. "I can't pass up such a delicious offer, but will you join us for a bite, too?"

Franny looked around the café. Seeing no customers needing her attention, she shrugged. "Sure, why not. It's not like I'm busy. If business keeps up like this, I might have to close down. I'll be back in a second with your pie and fresh coffee."

I glanced across the table at Candie. "Close down? What is she talking about? This restaurant has been her life since she moved north more than fifteen years ago."

Candie emptied her coffee mug. "I know. She came north about the same time I moved from Hainted Hollar. What would she do without Sweetie Pie's? I certainly can't picture her working for someone else when she's been her own boss for so long."

"It would be a tough one, especially since she was so successful with her own restaurant." I looked around the empty restaurant at the vacant booths and stools. This had to be a temporary situation, or at least, I hoped it was. Sweetie Pie's was usually packed from the moment it opened for the breakfast crowd to the last dinner patron.

"Here you go, ladies. I know you won't be disappointed. The recipe for the pie was my great-grandma's. A true Southern lady if there ever was one."

Candie frowned. Her ruby red fingernails tapped the tabletop.

Franny laughed. "Pardon me, Candie. You'd give her a run for her money in the Southern lady category."

Candie patted her curls. "Why thank you, Franny. I'm sure she was quite the Southern lady, too."

Franny slid the plates of banana cream pie before Candie and me then topped off our coffees.

Franny glanced around the restaurant then gave a dry laugh. "Let me grab a mug and pour myself some coffee. I'll be right back."

Within seconds, Franny returned to our booth with a steaming cup of coffee in her hand.

"Here, sit next to me." I slid farther down my booth seat.

"What do you think of the pie?" Franny asked, looking from Candie to me.

Candie rolled her eyes towards the ceiling and groaned. "Honey, are you sure you made this and not an angel?"

I reached behind Franny and rubbed her back. "Nope, I don't feel any angel wings sticking out. Must have been Franny who made this heavenly delight."

Franny laughed, but soon her laughter turned to tears. "Ladies, thank you. I needed that. It's the first time since Saturday I've felt like laughing."

I wrapped an arm around her shoulder and pulled her close to my side. "Oh, Franny. Things have been kind of crazy since then. I was at the police station earlier, and I overheard the finding of the lab report."

"You did? I know they suspect my barbeque of having lavender added to it to make people at the fair sick. I swear, neither Aaron, Joy, nor myself did anything to change the recipe I've been serving here in my restaurant for years. Can you tell me what the report said?" Franny reached across the table and yanked a napkin out of the metal dispenser. She swiped at the tears flowing down her smooth dark cheeks and blew her nose.

I squirmed in my seat. True, I wasn't sworn to silence about what I had overheard when leaving Hank's office, but would he be upset if I shared the information?

"Yes, the report mentioned lavender," I said.

"That's impossible." Franny clenched her fingers around her coffee mug's handle so tightly I thought it would snap off.

CHAPTER THIRTY-THREE

―――――

"I overheard the findings of the report as I was leaving the police station earlier today. Apparently, there was lavender mixed in with your pulled pork. Yours was the only one to contain it," I said. My heart broke as I relayed the information to Franny.

Franny swayed on the bench. I tightened my arm around her shoulder to steady her. I looked over to Candie. "Can you get her a glass of cold water? I'm afraid she's going to faint."

Candie slid across her bench and scurried over to the service station where waitresses kept water pitchers and coffee pots warming on burners handy for their customers. She grabbed a clean glass, filled it with water, and then hurried back to our table.

I took the glass from Candie and offered it to Franny. "Here, Franny, take a sip."

She reached out for the glass of water. Her slim hand was shaking so much that water splashed over the rim onto the table. I helped her guide it to her lips.

"Thank you," she said in a voice barely above a whisper.

She looked at me with her deep brown eyes. "It couldn't have been me who placed the lavender in the barbeque."

I took the glass from her hands and placed it on the table before her. "Why couldn't it have been?" Then I realized how harsh my statement was and clamped a hand over my mouth. "I'm not accusing you. If anything, I want to prove you innocent of harming people."

Candie reached across the table and folded Franny's hands in hers. "That's right, Sugar. Sam and I want to stop the ugly gossip going around town and see you proven innocent and Sweetie Pie's buzzing again. Even if it means we have to contend with lines of people in order to get in here."

Franny's lips turned up in a weak smile. She pulled a hand from Candie's and gave mine a gentle squeeze. "You two are the best, and I don't mean just as customers. I couldn't have put the lavender in the barbeque because I'm highly allergic to it—in any form. I can't go near it. I break out in a terrible rash and practically scratch the skin right off my bones it I come in contact with it."

"I'd say your allergy eliminates you, but what about Joy? Would she have done such a thing?" I hesitated to mention Aaron's name.

Franny gave her head a violent shake. She pounded the tabletop, causing the plates and mugs to jump. "No way. She knows of my allergy to lavender and wouldn't inflict such pain on her aunt. She loves me."

I squeezed her hand. "I know she loves you and wouldn't do anything to cause you harm. And from what I've observed of Aaron's and Joy's relationship, I don't think he'd do anything to damage it, either, and harming you or your business certainly would. I'd say it eliminates the three of you."

Franny looked at me with tears brimming in her eyes. "Yes, it eliminates me from trying to poison my customers, but the police still suspect me of murdering Edgar Jensen."

"Franny, Candie and I know you're not guilty of murdering him. You couldn't hurt a fly." An idea clicked in my head, and I was going to explore it. "In fact, we're going to go question the person who is on the top of my suspect list."

Candie's head jerked towards me. "What? Who? When? Where?"

I laughed. "You just asked a crime fighter's most important questions. Well, you did leave off the why, but we'll ask that, too."

Candie's forehead furrowed into a frown. "What are you talking about? Or should I say who?"

I picked up my fork and pointed it at Candie then dipped it into my pie. "Carol Jensen."

* * *

I pulled into Candie's driveway and turned off the Bug's ignition. "Are you up for visiting Carol tomorrow morning?"

Candie turned in her seat to face me. "Yes. I don't have to go in to work until noon, so I can make it." Wings Falls' budget could only afford a part-time secretary for the mayor, which suited Candie fine. It left her the time to write the romance novels she so loved and, lately, to help me with my sleuthing.

Mark's car was parked in the driveway in front of me. "It looks as if the Chamber of Commerce meeting must have ended early. You better hurry in to your bridegroom."

A smile spread across Candie's face. "Oh, goodie. And the night is still young." The expression on her face sobered. "Um, do you want to come in and say hi to him and see Dixie and Cuddles?"

Right, like it's what Mark has on his mind—my spending time with his pets. "No, I'd better get home to Porkchop. I'll pick you up at nine, and we'll head over to the Widow Jensen's house."

Candie leaned over and kissed my cheek then pushed her car door open. Before getting out of the car, she asked, "Are you going to call first and give her a heads-up we're coming over?"

I shook my head. "Nope. I want it to be a surprise."

"What's going to be your excuse for coming over?"

"I'll think of something. You know, paying our respects or something to that effect," I said.

Candie clapped her hands. "Oh, goodie. I'll wear something black and put on a real sad face at Edgar's passing. Night, sugar." Candie blew a kiss at me then shut the car door.

I rolled my eyes. I could see it now. Candie would be swooning with grief on Carol's sofa. Another Oscar-winning performance would be in the making.

I honked the car's horn and backed out of her driveway. I smiled as Mark opened the front door and pulled Candie into his arms. Yep, the night was still young for them. I thought of the long night that stretched out before me, but minus Hank. The little green devil named jealousy, inched its way through me. At least I did have my other main man—Porkchop—to keep me company.

*   *   *

I pulled my pillow over my head to block out the insistent buzzing in my ears. I reached out with my hand and searched for the source—my alarm clock. I fumbled around my nightstand but only managed to knock the clock onto the floor. Porkchop, awakened by the alarm, barked and bounced about the covers at my feet. I poked my head out from under my pillow. "Okay, okay. I'll get up. I need to drive over to Candie's and pick her up so we can head over to Carol Jensen's house." I leaned over my bed and rooted around the floor for my alarm clock. When I found it on top of my slippers, I punched off the alarm and returned it to its rightful place on my nightstand. Thankfully, my fuzzy slippers had cushioned its fall and the clock was none the worse for wear. I squinted at the time. Seven o'clock. Yep, time to get up, shower, dress, take care of Porkchop, grab a bagel, and head on over to Candie's to start our sleuthing.

After my shower, I threw on my best pair of black jeans and a black sweater. I figured if Candie was going to dress as a mourner, I should, too.

With Porkchop fed and let out, I gobbled down my sesame seed bagel and a cup of decaf. I snatched my keys from the kitchen counter, where I had tossed them last night when I arrived home from dropping off Candie. Porkchop sat on the kitchen floor and looked up at me with sad eyes. I bent and scratched him between his ears. "Porkchop, I won't be away as long today, I promise. I have to call Jane Burrows to make sure the book reading and signing I have scheduled when our book is released is still scheduled." When Jane, the head librarian at our town's library, first heard of Porkchop's and my book being published, she asked me to do a children's hour at the library. Of course, I said yes, thrilled at the thought of sharing *Porkchop, the Wonder Dog,* with others.

"If you're a good boy, I'll stop at the butcher on my way home and buy you a tasty bone."

Porkchop wagged his tail at the mention of "bone."

I blew him a kiss and set out for Candie's, ready to prove Carol Jensen was responsible for her husband's murder.

CHAPTER THIRTY-FOUR

———

Candie bounded out of the house as soon as I pulled to a stop in her driveway. I stifled a laugh. She was dressed in a gauzy black skirt with a matching black top. Clear rhinestones rimmed the neckline. Leave it to my cousin to add bling even to a somber outfit. She once told me when the angels took her to the Good Lord in heaven, she wanted her coffin trimmed with the largest rhinestones a person could find.

She pulled open the passenger-side door and slid into the seat. I got a closer look at the black cowboy boots she'd paired with her outfit. This time I did laugh out loud. Rhinestones ran down the sides of her boots.

Candie looked at me wide-eyed. "What? What's the matter? Is my lipstick smudged or something? I told Mark not to mess it up when he gave me a kiss goodbye, but he didn't listen to me. He said he wanted to give me a kiss I'd remember until I got to the office this afternoon." She waved her bejeweled fingers in front of her face to cool herself down.

I smiled. "You've only been married four months. Mark is still on his honeymoon, as I'm sure you are, too."

Candie blushed. "You're right about that, sugar. I'd be tickled pink if this honeymoon never ends."

"Knowing you, I'm sure it won't." I shifted into reverse and backed out of Candie's driveway. I headed the Bug towards Widow Jensen's house.

* * *

On the way to Carol's house, I stopped at Blooms Florist and purchased a bouquet of carnations. I needed some excuse to drop in on her. I felt flowers were a standard gift when a person passed away.

We sat in Carol's driveway staring at her house. The beat-up car that waited impatiently for our parking spot at Discount World the other day was parked before a garage door whose paint was flaking off. The rest of the house wasn't in much better shape than the garage. Paint peeled off the front door, and shutters hung drunkenly from the windows.

Candie stared wide-eyed out the front window. "How did you find her address?"

"You can find anything on the internet. After I got home yesterday, I googled her, and this is what popped up. Not much to look at, is it?"

Candie shook her head. "I'm surprised. No, I'm shocked. With the position Edgar held at the bank, I thought he'd live in a fancy house."

I reached into the back seat for flowers then opened my door. "Ready to do a bit of sleuthing?"

Candie flung her auburns curls over her shoulder. "Lead on, Cagney."

I laughed. Candie was referring to the old television show, *Cagney and Lacey*, from the 80s. Earlier in the year, when we were trying to find the killer of her ex-fiancé, she wanted to be Lacey and I was to be Cagney. "We'll have to be plain old Candie and Sam. I'm sure she'll remember us from the fair on Saturday."

Candie pouted. "You're no fun."

I slid out of the car and motioned for her to follow me. "Come on. Let's get this over with."

As we walked up to the house, I noticed weeds growing between the cracked cement of the walkway.

"Oops!" Candie jerked forward and clutched on to the sleeve of my sweater.

I grabbed her arm. "What's the matter?"

Candie regained her balance and brushed back a strand of hair that had fallen over her face. "I tripped on a loose piece of cement. This place needs major repair."

I nodded. "I noticed that as soon as I pulled into the driveway. For someone who held such a good position at the bank, I'm surprised at the condition of the Jensen's home."

Candie ran a hand through her hair. "Yeah, it looks like Edgar wasn't exactly Joe the Handyman."

We arrived at the front door, and I drew in a deep breath. With the bouquet clutched in one hand, I knocked on the dented metal door with the other.

Through the door, I heard a game show blasting from a television. I turned to Candie and raised an eyebrow.

"I'm coming. I'm coming. Hold your horses."

My mouth dropped open at the sight that greeted us when the door opened. Carol stood before us in a *very* short nightgown. Her flaming red hair hung in a wild mess about her shoulders.

"What do you ladies want? If you're collecting for some church, I gave up on your God years ago. He ain't helped me since I don't know when."

Shouting and clapping came from the living room. Carol turned her head in the direction of the television. Someone must have won big on the game show she'd been watching.

Candie leaned toward me and whispered, "I guess she never heard the phrase 'The Lord helps those who help themselves.'"

Candie stepped back to avoid the jab I tried to deliver to her ribs. Now wasn't the time to judge Carol. We had more important matters to address.

I held the carnations out to Carol when she returned her attention to us. "We wanted to stop by and offer our condolences at the loss of your husband."

Carol blinked then reached for the flowers. "That's mighty kind of you." She squinted her eyes. "Do I know you ladies? You do look kind of familiar. Where do I know you from?"

"You might have seen us at the Taste of Wings Falls on Saturday," I said, hoping to be invited into the house so we could ask more questions. I didn't want to quiz her on her doorstep. "Umm, do you have a vase to put the flowers in?"

Carol looked at the flowers clutched in her hand as if she just realized she held them. "Oh, right, the flowers. I know I have a vase somewhere. I'll have to go look."

I snatched at this as our opportunity to be invited inside. "Can we give you a hand? I know you must be very distraught right now and probably not thinking straight."

Candie and I followed Carol inside as she went in search of a vase for the flowers.

"Suzy Homemaker she's not," Candie said as we stood gazing around the living room.

Shabby didn't begin to describe it. I wondered if the dump would even take her sofa, with its torn cushion and springs poking out. A coffee table stood before it with a pile of books acting as one of its legs. Center stage across from the sofa was a fifty-inch flat-screen television, the source of the game show we'd heard through the front door. A lamp, minus its shade, resided on a scarred table next to the sofa.

I raised an eyebrow at what the table held and pointed to a half-empty bottle of wine and a full glass of the vino. "It isn't even ten o'clock!"

Candie shrugged. "As they say—it's five o'clock somewhere."

Another item caught my attention on the table. I walked over, picked up the pile, and held it for Candie to see. "Scratch-off lotto tickets?" I fanned them out in my hand. "There has to be at least a couple dozen here. That's quite a gambling habit."

"Didn't Patsy Ikeda say she saw Carol at the Racino? Frank said she got upset with Edgar at the fair when he didn't win that teddy bear for her," Candie said.

I quickly replaced the lotto cards on the table as I heard Carol returning to the living room. When she entered, my nose detected a scent that was all too familiar.

CHAPTER THIRTY-FIVE

———

"Lavender," I whispered to Candie.

She gave me a clueless look. "What?" she whispered back.

I wanted to shake my cousin. "Don't you get it? Lavender was found in Franny's pulled pork."

"Ohhhh," Candie breathed out.

"Thank you, ladies, for these beautiful flowers. It was very kind of you. I'll put the flowers on my coffee table so I can enjoy how pretty they are whenever I'm watching my shows." She placed a chipped blue glass vase in the middle of the table then sat to admire them. After a tug at the hem of her nightgown, not that it did any good, she reached over and picked up her glass of wine. Before raising it to her lips, she said, "Oh, my, where's my manners? Would you two like a glass?"

Candie and I both declined. I pointed to the stack of lotto cards. "Any winners there?" I said it with a laugh so she'd think I was only curious and not prying for something deeper.

She twirled her wineglass between her fingers. "Oh, it's a little hobby of mine."

Candie pointed to the table with a bejeweled finger. "Wouldn't buying so many cards get a little pricey?"

I groaned silently. Leave it to my cousin to get right to the point. I hoped she hadn't made Carol wary of why we were here.

Carol took another sip of her wine and shook her head. "Now, with Edgar gone, I'm going to have to cut back on playing the lotto." She gave a disgruntled laugh. "Anyway, the state has these games rigged. I really should give it up all together." She reached over for the wine bottle and topped off her glass.

While I might not indulge in alcohol this early in the morning, it seemed to be making Carol's tongue loose, for which I was very grateful.

"Why does Edgar's death mean you have to cut back on buying your lotto tickets?" I asked.

Carol swallowed another sip of wine. "He had a little fund I used to buy them with, but now that he's dead, I won't be able to do that anymore."

Candie leaned towards me and mouthed, *The "special fee"?*

I agreed. It looked like the fee he charged people for their loans funded Carol's gambling habit. Poor guy. I wondered if he knew his dear wife was cheating on him, too. If so, why would he have acted so foolishly? Like people said—love was blind, but then maybe they had what some people called an…open marriage. She put up with his flirtations as long as she got money to gamble and maybe a fling or two on her part.

I noticed a large bandage crisscrossing the top of her left hand. "Did you hurt yourself?" I nodded towards her injured hand.

She stared down at her hand as if she'd just noticed the bandage. "Oh, that. A wineglass slipped and broke when I was washing it yesterday. Clumsy me. A piece of the glass sliced me while I was cleaning it up. The cut isn't anything, though." A nervous laugh escaped her lips.

Carol reached for a small vial sitting on the table next to the wine bottle. She unscrewed the top and tried to pour a small amount onto the palm of her hand. It slipped and rolled onto the sofa, spilling its contents onto a cushion crisscrossed with duct tape. The scent of lavender filled the room.

Carol brushed at the oil soaking into the cushion. "Drat. That's the last bottle I have. I'll have to stop by Montana's shop and buy some more."

This was my chance to quiz her. "I bought a vial of lavender from Montana on Saturday at the fair. Did you purchase some from her?"

Carol's head jerked up. "Hmmm, why yes, I did."

Candie placed a hand on my arm. "Let me ask the next question. Why did you put lavender into Franny Goodway's pulled pork?"

Whoa, nothing like getting to the point!

Carol swayed on the cushion. I didn't know if it was from all the wine she had consumed or the shock of Candie's question. She slammed her wineglass on the table. "That woman! Her niece was trying to seduce my Edgar. There was no way I would see her win any contest." Spittle drooled down her chin.

Oops. Maybe she wasn't so forgiving of Edgar's peccadilloes.

Now it was my turn to speak. "Carol, your husband made an unwanted pass at Joy. You had no right to do such a thing. What you did made a number of people sick and has caused damage to Franny's business. I'm going to report what you said to the police."

Carol rose from the sofa. She grabbed on to the arm for support. The wine had taken its toll on her equilibrium. She jabbed the air with a shaking finger. Anger oozed forth from her body. "Get out! Get out of my house! If you say anything to the police, I'll deny it."

Candie and I backed out of the house. I was afraid to turn my back on the raging woman. I heard her cursing us all the way to my Bug.

We sat in my car and stared at each other. "What do you think?" Candie asked.

"We solved one mystery—who put the lavender in Franny's barbeque." I turned and shoved my key into the ignition.

Candie buckled her seat belt. "Do you think Hank can arrest her?"

I placed the car in reverse, happy to pull out of the driveway. "I don't know. There weren't any witnesses, and as Carol said, it would be her word against ours."

Candie's phone rang out from her purse. She reached in and pulled out the bejeweled phone. She smiled and swiped across its surface. She turned to me and mouthed, *Mark.* "Hi, sweetie, I'll have Sam drop me off at work in a few minutes. What? The animal shelter?... Cuddles? What happened? Is he all right?"

Candie's hand shook as she disconnected. She sat in her seat and stared at the phone.

I pulled over to the side of the road. "What did Mark want? You said the animal shelter. You mean For Pet's Sake? For Cuddles? It can't be anything terrible. If Cuddles was sick or hurt, Mark would have us go to the Wings Falls Animal Hospital."

By now Candie's whole body shook with deep sobs. "Mark wouldn't say. He just told me to get there right away. Oh, Sam, I'm scared."

I put my car in gear and pulled out onto the road. "We'll go right now. Mystery will be solved, and you'll see everything is all right."

* * *

I spied Mark's car when we pulled into the For Pet's Sake parking lot. I pulled up next to it. Candie was out the door before I even turned off the Bug's engine. I grabbed my purse and raced into the building after her. What greeted me when I entered the cinder block building stopped me in my tracks. A family of four, what I took to be a mother, father, young son and daughter, were fawning over Cuddles. The children sat on the tile floor and squealed when Cuddles jumped from one child's lap to the other, licking their faces. Mark and Shirley stood to the side, watching. Mark fiddled nervously with Cuddles's sparkly leash in his hands. Candie looked on as if in a trance.

I walked over to Shirley. "What's going on? How come those people have Cuddles?"

She shook her head. A tear rolled down her face. Now I knew something bad was happening. Shirley was one of the least emotional women I knew. If there was a poster child for "tough as nails," Shirley would be it.

"That's the Peabody family. They were camping locally three weeks ago, and Foster got away from them. They looked everywhere for him but finally had to give up their search and return home."

I pointed to the boy who was now rolling on the floor with the dog jumping on him. "You mean Cuddles, umm Foster belongs to them?"

CHAPTER THIRTY-SIX

———

Shirley nodded. "They subscribe to the online version of the *Tribune* and saw the pictures of the Taste. They recognized their dog from the photo Rob Anderson took of Candie and Cuddles at the Loopy Ladies' booth on Saturday."

"How can they be sure Cuddles is their Foster?" Candie asked, desperation filling her voice. "They could be saying that to get a free dog."

"Follow me," Shirley said, waving us over to a counter used as the reception desk. She picked up a photo and handed it to me. Candie remained with Mark. She probably didn't want to see any proof that Cuddles wasn't hers.

I gazed down at it. It did look like Cuddles, but then, there could be a bazillion dogs that looked like him.

Shirley tapped the picture. I zeroed in on what she pointed to. I gave her a questioning look.

"Don't you see?" she asked. "Cuddles has an extra toe on his left hind foot. You can see it clearly in this picture."

"I never noticed it." I walked over to Cuddles and bent to examine his foot. Sure enough, I spotted an extra toe.

A deep sob behind me caused me to turn to Candie. She was weeping into Mark's chest. I walked over and placed my hand on her back. "Candie, I'm so sorry. I know you didn't have Cuddles for long, but you loved him with all of your heart."

Candie lifted her head from Mark's chest and swiped at her tears. "What am I going to tell Dixie? She and Cuddles have become so close. This will break her heart."

"I know, sweetheart. In such a short time, all of you welcomed Cuddles into your hearts. But think about it, if you hadn't rescued him the other day, what would have happened to him? You saved him from who knows what."

A faint smile curved Candie's lips. "I did, didn't I?"

I nodded and turned to the family. "Yes, you did. You can see the family loves him as much as you do." I pointed to the young girl laughing and hugging Cuddles to her.

Candie took Cuddles's leash from Mark's hand and walked over to the couple watching their children play with the dog. She cleared her throat and held out the leash. "I bought this for Cuddles—or rather, Foster—on Saturday. I'd like him to have it as a little reminder of how much I love him."

The mother shook her head. "Oh, no. I couldn't do that. It must be very expensive."

Candie pressed the leash into the woman's hand. "Please, I insist. It will make me feel better knowing he's wearing the collar and you're using the leash I bought him. I'll feel like he has a part of me still with him." Candie leaned down and gave Cuddles a pat then turned to Mark. "Come on. Let's go home."

Mark led a sobbing Candie out the shelter's door and to his car.

I said goodbye to Shirley and gave Cuddles one last pat. "We'll miss you," I whispered into his ear. I pushed open the shelter's heavy metal door and walked to my car. Mark was pulling out of his parking space. Candie sat besides him, her face buried in her hands while her body shook with sobs.

Mark rolled down his window as I opened the Bug's door. "Thank you for being there for Candie."

"Of course. Tell her to call when she's feeling up to it."

He agreed, and then we both drove out of the shelter's parking lot and headed towards home.

As I drove, I remembered I had promised Porkchop a bone from the butcher shop. It would only be about a ten-minute detour, and a promise was a promise.

* * *

A bell jangled over the Meat of the Matter Butcher Shop's door, announcing my entry. I waved to the store's owner, Angelo Condi, a portly gentleman wearing a long white apron, who happened to be Gladys's brother. Posters of cuts of meat decorated the wall behind him. This was my go-to shop for Porkchop's bones. Plus, he sold the best cuts of meat in town.

"What can I do for you, Sam?" he asked.

"I need a good-sized bone as a treat for my dog," I replied. "I don't see any in your display case."

He chuckled. "I keep those in a refrigerator in the back. Let me go fetch one for you. You must have one special pup."

"I do," I said as he went to get the bone for Porkchop.

The shop's bell jangled again. I turned to see who had entered.

I greeted Bill Collins as he approached the counter. "Hi, Bill. What happened to your hand?" His right hand was heavily bandaged.

He blinked and held out his hand in front of him. "Umm, an accident at the restaurant. No big deal."

He was the third person I'd seen with a hand wound. First, Aaron said he burned himself while cooking. Second, Carol Jensen cut her hand while washing a wineglass. Third, Bill had a "no big deal" accident at his restaurant. That seemed like a crazy coincidence. An idea formed in my brain. Could the blood on Porkchop's paws have been from one of these three people? I hoped and prayed it wasn't Aaron or Bill, but Carol? She did like her wine, and maybe she got drunk and had an argument with Edgar. She could have accidentally pushed the pumpkin on him in the heat of the moment. She was back at the top of my suspect list for Edgar's murder.

Angelo returned with a large bone. He wrapped it, and then I paid him and left the shop. As I walked past Bill, I told him to take care of his hand so it wouldn't become infected. He said he would. The bell over the door jangled once again as I left the shop with Porkchop's bone clutched in my hand.

Within minutes, I pulled into my driveway. I turned off the car and sat gazing at my ranch-style home. I thought of what waited to greet me behind my front door—my loving and cuddly Porkchop. I dreaded the day it would not be a reality. Pets wormed their way into your life and stole your heart. They became family. I grieved for Candie. She may only have had Cuddles for a few days, but he had already become a part of her and Mark's family. Cuddles and Porkchop were like the children we were never blessed with.

I opened my car door, and sure enough, as I approached my front door, I heard Porkchop barking on the other side. How he knew it was me, I had no idea, but he did. He jumped at my legs when I opened the door.

I placed his bone on the table in my entryway then bent and scooped him into my arms. I hugged him close. I never wanted to let him go.

Porkchop squealed so I placed him on the floor. "All right, all right. I guess that's enough loving. You want your kibble, and I didn't forget the bone I promised you."

At the mention of the word "kibble," he raced ahead of me into the kitchen. I picked his bone-shaped bowl off the floor and filled it with his food. At the sound of his food plinking into the bowl, he barked and his tail wagged.

My phone rang. I dug it out of my black jeans' back pocket. Was it only this morning Candie and I dressed in funeral black to visit the Widow Jensen? I needed to let Hank know about her being the person who messed with Franny's barbeque. Not that I thought it would do any good. As Carol had said, it was her word against mine. I didn't know if I'd tell him about my suspicions concerning the three people with hand wounds just yet. I wanted to do a little more digging.

I glanced at the caller ID and smiled—Hank. I swiped my phone and answered. "I was just thinking about you."

"Sexy thoughts, I hope," Hank said, his voice lowered to a sultry tone that made my toes tingle.

I chuckled. "Well, not exactly. I wanted to tell you about Candie's and my visit with Carol Jensen this morning."

"You went to see her?"

I could picture his eye roll at my statement.

"Yes, we did and found out who added the lavender to Franny's pulled pork."

"Hold that thought. I'll make reservations at The Round Up for dinner and pick you up at six."

I had a suspicion this was not going to be a leisurely dinner. Hank was going to do a little snooping of his own while we ate.

Hank and I exchanged a few more words then hung up.

I looked down at Porkchop sitting at my feet. "Porkie, Hank's coming over and we're going out to eat." Porkchop barked and bounced on his short legs. "I'm sorry, sweetie, you're not included. It's going to be just Hank and me." I cradled his small head in my hands. "But if we're lucky, maybe he'll spend the night."

I looked down at the black outfit I had donned this morning to visit Carol. "I need to shower and change. Enough of doom and gloom. I want to push all thoughts of Edgar's death out of my mind and enjoy myself tonight. Let's see what happy outfit I can dig out of my closet."

Porkchop followed me to my bedroom. I opened the door to the room where I had spent my childhood. I had made a few changes over the years, especially since I started seeing Hank. I'd replaced my twin bed with a queen, added a soft gray comforter, and donated the purple with white polka dots one to the Salvation Army. My Donnie Osmond poster was gone from the ceiling. It must have unnerved Hank to have "a little bit of rock n' roll" staring down on him when I snuggled in his arms.

The maple dresser from my youth stood on the far wall. No use replacing a solid dresser. I walked over to my closet and slid open the door. "Okay, any suggestions, Porkchop?" He tilted his head.

"How about this?" I asked, sliding an orange sweater out for his inspection.

He barked his approval.

"Okay, I'll pair it with jeans that hug my body in all the right places. Now for a shower."

CHAPTER THIRTY-SEVEN

———

The sound of car tires crunching on my driveway announced Hank's Jeep pulling into my driveway promptly at six o'clock. I wasn't the only one aware of his arrival. Porkchop, who had been enjoying his bone in front of the fireplace, perked up his ears then raced to the front door, beating me to it.

Before Hank could knock on the door, I opened it. He stood with his fist raised, ready to announce his arrival. "You look beautiful."

Heat crawled up my neck. I still wasn't used to his compliments. My ex had rarely paid me any. I walked towards him, and he hugged me close then bent his head and placed a gentle but sizzling kiss on my lips.

I pulled back, breathing heavily. "Are you sure you want to go out to dinner? I can always order in pizza. I have a couple of Trail's Heads in the fridge," I said, mentioning his favorite beer.

Hank shook his head. The wayward curl fell over his forehead. "I promised you a dinner out, and I always keep my promises."

I reached up and pushed back this curl with a mind of its own. "I know you do. It's one of the many things I love about you."

Hank ran a finger along my cheek. "Many things? How many are there? Do you want to elaborate?"

I playfully jabbed his shoulder. "I don't want you to get a big head. Besides, I'm hungry."

He looked down at me with a pout on his lips. "Okay. Grab your coat and let's go."

I stepped out of his arms and walked to the coat closet. I grabbed a heavy jacket, anticipating cooler temperatures when we left The Round Up.

"Let, me get my purse and give Porkchop a handful of kibble."

"Okay." Hank gave Porkchop a parting scratch between the ears.

* * *

"I'm glad I made reservations. This place is really hopping tonight," Hank said as he pulled his Jeep into one of the last parking spaces in The Round Up's lot.

I looked around the packed parking area. "It looks like what happened at the fair didn't affect his business like it did Franny's."

Hank looked at me. "Once we're inside and settled at our table, I want you to tell me all about your snooping at Carol Jensen's today."

I fidgeted with the door handle. "It wasn't snooping. Candie and I were sleuthing."

"Whatever. Let's enjoy our meal before we discuss your antics today." Hank stepped out of the car then walked around to open the door on my side.

The sound of happy diners hit our ears when we stepped into The Round Up. Bill Collins, dressed in his usual western-style shirt and jeans, stood by the hostess station talking to a young woman outfitted in a denim shirt and tight-fitting jeans. A red-checked bandana was tied around her neck. "Evening, Hank, Sam. How are you doing tonight? I hope you have reservations. As you can see, we're packed tonight. But you are two of my favorite customers, so I'll always squeeze you in." Bill turned to the hostess, who checked off our reservations on the large book spread out before her. "Claire, I'll show them to their table."

Hank glanced around the room. "You certainly are busy tonight, and it's not even the weekend."

Bill chuckled. "Folks know where to come for good food and entertainment. The Sundowners are taking the stage later on. Will you hang around to hear them?"

"Don't you usually have bands only on the weekends?" I asked, following behind Bill.

He nodded. "Yes, but I thought I'd liven the place up a bit tonight and asked them to play."

Over the years, household names like Willie, Dolly, and Crystal, to name a few, had also performed here. Their pictures decorated the rough pine walls.

Bill pointed to a round oak table situated next to the stage. "How's this? Right next to the stage in case you decide to hang around until showtime."

"Thanks, Bill. Looks like you did a number on your hand. What did you do?" Hank asked, pulling out my chair.

"Oh, that. It's nothing." Bill covered his bandaged hand with the other. "I was trimming back some brush in my yard and slipped with my saw. Real clumsy of me. I have some business to attend to. Enjoy your meal."

I shook my head and frowned as I watched him hurry to the back of the restaurant.

Hank pulled out his chair and sat. "Why the frown? Something the matter?"

"I ran into Bill at the Meat of the Matter Butcher Shop today and asked him about his hand. He told me he cut it here at The Round Up." I wondered about his change in story.

Hank unwrapped the red napkin holding his silverware and placed it on his lap. "That is strange, but maybe he cut his hand here and reinjured it at home or vice versa."

I did the same with my napkin. "I guess so." But I wasn't entirely convinced. Something else about Bill niggled at me, too. I just couldn't put my finger on it yet. I glanced around the room. Not much had changed since Bill's father opened the restaurant in the 50s. The same wood wagon wheel chandeliers hung from the ceiling. The restroom doors were still labeled Cowboys and Cowgirls. It was reassuring that some things hadn't changed with the times. I hoped they could make whatever improvements the restaurant needed and not affect the homey atmosphere it had.

Hank leaned across the table. "Okay, now spill it."

I gave him my best wide-eyed, *what do you mean* look. "Spill what? What are you talking about?"

Hank leaned back in his chair. He was so handsome in the baby blue sweater he wore. It was the exact color of his eyes. "Saaammm," he said, drawing out my name. "This afternoon. The little trip you and Candie took to Carol Jensen's house."

My mouth formed an *O*. "Oh, that."

Hank steepled his fingers under his chin. "Yeah, that."

"You folks care to see a menu, or do you know what you'd like?"

My head jerked up to see our young waitress standing next to our table, holding a stack of plastic-coated menus in her arms.

"Oh hi, Jennifer." She had waited on us previously when we'd dined here. "I really enjoyed the barbeque sampler platter I had here last time. I think I'll try it again."

"Sure," she said, juggling the menus and pulling out an order pad from her back pocket. She tugged a pencil from behind her ear and turned to Hank with it poised over the pad.

"I'll have the same, and add a Trail's Head for me. Sam, would you care for a drink?"

I looked up at Jennifer. "I think I'd like a glass of Riesling."

Jennifer tucked the order pad back into her pocket and stuck the pencil back over her ear. "Great, I'll hand in your orders and be back right away with your drinks."

Jennifer was back in minutes. The sounds of happy diners and piped-in country music floated around us. I twirled the stem of my glass in my fingers. "Okay, where should I start?"

"How about at the beginning," Hank said, clutching his beer bottle in his strong hands.

I nodded. "I know you told me Carol had an alibi for the time of her husband's death, but I couldn't shake the feeling she was involved, somehow, in Saturday's events, whether it was Edgar's death or the people getting sick at the fair."

"So, did this 'feeling' of yours pan out?"

I stared at the wine in my glass, wishing I had a better answer. "Yes, it did, but I'm afraid it's my word against hers."

CHAPTER THIRTY-EIGHT

———

I took a sip of my wine then proceeded to tell Hank all about Candie's and my trip to Carol's house.

"So, she confessed to you two that she poured the lavender into Franny's pulled pork?"

I looked across the table at Hank and nodded. "Yes, but how can we prove it? She said she'd deny everything."

Hank looked around him. In a lowered voice, he said, "I got a call from the bank today. They are looking into Edgar's loan practices. It seems they've uncovered some irregularities, and Carol was the recipient of some of the money he extorted out of loan applicants. I'll bet she'd rather plead guilty to messing with Franny's barbeque than to bank fraud."

I clapped my hands. "Really, Hank? That would clear Franny's name, and people would flock back to Sweetie Pie's."

He placed a finger to his lips and glanced around the crowded room. "Shhh. We don't want to alert her. I'll place a call to the station right now and have an officer drive over to her house and question her." He pulled his phone out of the back pocket of his jeans and pushed the button for the police station. After relaying the information I had given him, he hung up. And just in time. Jennifer arrived with our dinners.

"Can I get you anything else? Another drink?" she asked after placing our meals in front of us.

Hank looked at me.

"No, thanks. I'm fine for now," I said, pointing to my half-full glass of wine.

* * *

Hank leaned back in his seat and let out a sigh. "Just as good as the last time we ate here."

"My meal was fabulous. If there was a barbeque rematch with the three restaurants from the fair on Saturday, I don't know if I could have picked a winner. Each of them has their own particular flavor." I laughed. "I love them all."

I placed my napkin on the table and pushed back my chair. "I'm afraid I need to go to the Cowgirl's room. I'll be back in a minute." I walked over to Hank and placed a kiss on his cheek.

"Okay, I'll settle up with Jennifer while you're gone."

On my way back from the Cowgirl's room, I noticed the door to Bill's office was cracked open and saw him sitting at his desk talking on the phone. His change of story about how he injured his hand bothered me. I wanted to see what he'd say if I questioned him about it.

I pushed the door open and waved to Bill. He motioned for me to come in. He ended his phone call and got up from his desk, walking around it.

"Hi, Sam. I hope you and Hank enjoyed your meal. I'm glad you had reservations. As you can see, we are really busy tonight."

"Yes, thankfully Hank thought to call ahead. Ummm, I was wondering, at the butcher shop today you told me you hurt your hand here at the restaurant, but you told Hank it was a gardening accident… Why the change of stories?"

Bill started to stutter. His face turned red. He ran a hand through his thinning gray hair. That's when I noticed it—a safety pin held his cuff together where there should have been a shiny pearl button—matching the one I'd found in my car.

"You didn't hurt you hand in either of those situations, did you? You were at Eagle Drugs, weren't you, and my dog, Porkchop, bit you. What did you do to him to make him lash out at you? He's never bitten a soul before."

My anger was rising. My momma bear protection instinct concerning Porkchop was erupting. What had Bill done to my poor pup to make him bite his hand? Fortunately, except for the blood on his paws, I hadn't seen any injury to Porkchop.

"Sam, you don't know when to stop poking your nose in other people's business. I thought if I borrowed your dog for a while, you'd get the hint to leave things well enough alone. But your fool dog wouldn't cooperate. He took a good bite out of my hand."

I had to smile. Good for Porkchop for defending himself, and then my mouth dropped open and it dawned on me. "The only reason you don't want me to keep asking questions is because you're involved in Edgar Jensen's murder, aren't you?"

Bill's face turned white. I had hit the proverbial nail on the head. "Why did you kill him, Bill? I know you needed a loan to make the needed repairs to your restaurant, but you could have gone to another bank, like Clint Higgins."

Bill's shoulders slumped. A tear ran down his weathered face. "You don't understand. This restaurant has been in my family since the 50s. My dad started it. It's all I have to leave to my sons. Edgar Jensen didn't care about any of that. All he wanted was his 'special fee.' I was driving past the park on Saturday night and saw him taking a walk. I got out of my car, and well, one thing led to another, and we started arguing. I was so mad, I gave him a good push. Unfortunately, he stumbled and fell up against that dang pumpkin. Next thing I know, it landed on him. I know I should have called 9-1-1, but I panicked and left. I didn't mean to kill him. Honest I didn't."

Bill turned and leaned heavily on his paper-strewn desk.

My heart ached for him. Edgar Jensen had wreaked havoc on a lot of people, destroying so many lives.

Bill straightened up and spun around to face me, a letter opener clutched in his hand. "Sam, you can't tell anyone what I've just told you. You can't. It would ruin everything for my boys."

I backed up, but the back of my legs hit a chair and there was nowhere to go. I put my hands up in front of me to ward off a possible attack—like they would do any good.

Bill circled the desk. I was trapped. His eyes glazed over with a wild look. White spittle drooled out of the corners of his mouth. I wondered if he even knew where he was.

"Bill, please. Harming me won't do you, your sons, or the restaurant any good. You'll be guilty of two murders."

"I'll tell Hank that you received a phone call from a concerned neighbor saying they saw smoke coming from your house. In your panic to get back to your table to tell him, you'll have a little accident. Oh, my, how tragic. You tripped and fell on this letter opener, and unfortunately it plunged right into your heart. So sad."

Clearly, the man was in a crazed state. "Bill please, you don't have to do this," I pleaded. Images of Porkchop and Hank flashed before me. Were these going to be my last thoughts before I was killed?

"Sorry, Sam, but I do." He raised the letter opener, took a step towards me, and aimed it at my chest.

"Sam, are you in there? What's happening?"

The sound of Hank's voice momentarily caught Bill off guard, and he swiveled towards the door. I lunged towards his desk and grabbed the only lethal object I could find to disarm him—a metal stapler. I picked it up and threw it at his head.

Bill stumbled and fell to the floor, groaning as he clutched his head.

Hank pushed the door open and scanned the room to see Bill slumped on the floor. The letter opener had flown out of his hand and lay at Hank's feet. He bent and picked it up. "Care to tell me what happened on your way to the Cowgirl's room?"

My knees wobbled from the aftermath of what had happened. I sank into the chair. Hank walked over and knelt beside me. Bill was no longer a threat to me as he lay curled in a ball on the floor, sobbing.

I pointed to Bill. "He killed Edgar."

Hank stood and pulled his phone out of his pocket. He dialed the station and requested an officer to come to The Round Up. After hanging up, he helped Bill to his feet and over to the chair behind the desk and read him his rights.

Saddened by what had happened to this once feisty man, I asked, "Can I get your sons for you?"

Bill's head jerked up. "No," he said in a strong voice. "I don't want my foolishness interrupting business." Gone was the crazed look in his eyes from moments before. He seemed to have returned to a more rational frame of mind.

Bill was a one of a kind. I looked over at Hank. "Could we meet the officer you called outside the restaurant so the diners won't know what has happened in here?"

Hank nodded. "Bill, will you cooperate with me? You can call your lawyer and have him meet us at the station."

Bill looked from Hank to me. A deep sadness clouded his eyes. "Yeah. I didn't mean to kill him. It was an accident."

Hank placed a hand on Bill's shoulder. "I know you didn't, and hopefully that will go a long way with the judge and jury. Come on, let's meet that police car outside." Hank placed a hand under Bill's elbow and helped him out of his seat.

CHAPTER THIRTY-NINE

———

"Has it been a week since we were all gathered around your fire pit?" Candie asked.

I nodded. "What a week it was, too. Hank, have you heard how things are going with Bill Collins?"

The fire roared in my fire pit. Hank, Candie, and I sat hugging the warmth from the flames shooting out of it, sipping hot chocolate. Nina and Porkchop lay at our feet chewing on rawhide bones. Dixie sat curled on Candie's lap. Mark had dropped Dixie and Candie off then said he'd be back in a bit. He had an errand to run.

"The last I heard, he has a good lawyer, and hopefully, the judge and jury will go easy on him, although he is facing an involuntary-manslaughter charge."

My heart sank at this news. Yes, a person had died, but he had tried to destroy others' lives for his greed. I guess it was a good thing I wasn't judge or jury. I'd have strung Edgar up by his toes for all he had done.

"And Carol. What will become of her?" Candie asked, running her fingers through Dixie's fur.

Hank tossed a stick into the flames. Sparks rose to the heavens. "When faced with the bank charges, she confessed to putting the lavender in Franny's barbeque. That's another one we'll have to wait for the courts to decide."

Candie looked up from stroking Dixie's head. "At least Franny was absolved of any wrongdoing."

I smiled. "Yes. I stopped in there earlier, and Sweetie Pie's was packed. Aaron was busy in the kitchen, and Joy was hopping from customer to customer."

I placed a hand on Hank's arm. "Has Aaron decided whether he's going to go to school for culinary arts?"

A smile crept across his face. "Yeah, he finally made up his mind to make something out of his life. He's enrolled for the winter term. And to sweeten things for him, Joy is going, too."

I clapped my hands in excitement. "Goodie. I knew you were a good influence on him."

Red crawled up Hank's face, and I didn't think it was from the fire we were sitting next to. "I believe it was more of the influence of a good woman than anything I did."

"Hi, folks. I'm back."

We all turned to see Mark walk towards us. He clutched a squirming bundle of fur in his arms.

Candie placed Dixie on the ground and walked towards him. "Sweetie, what do you have there?"

He placed the little fur ball on the ground.

Candie dropped to her knees and gathered the dog to her. "What? Where? How?"

Mark knelt next to her. Dixie sat beside them, looking from one of her parents to the other. "Shirley called me and said Cuddles had a girlfriend and got her preggers. This is one of her pups. She asked if we'd like one, and I said definitely. What do you want to name her?"

Candie thought for a moment then said, "Annie. Definitely, Annie." She turned to Dixie. "What do you make of your new sister?" Dixie ambled over to Annie and licked her face.

I turned to Hank. "I guess this is a perfect ending to the week."

Hank shook his head and pulled me close to him. He whispered next to my lips, "No, this is." Then he kissed me.

ABOUT THE AUTHOR

Syrl Ann Kazlo, a retired teacher, lives in upstate New York with her husband and two very lively dachshunds. Kibbles and Death is the first book in her Samantha Davies Mystery series, featuring Samantha Davies and her lovable dachshund, Porkchop. When not writing Syrl is busy hooking—rug hooking that is—reading, and enjoying her family. She is a member of Sisters in Crime and the Mavens of Mayhem.

Learn more about S.A. Kazlo at:
www.sakazlo.com

Made in United States
Cleveland, OH
24 November 2024